Orphan Child

Omar Dixon

iUniverse, Inc.
Bloomington

ORPHAN CHILD

iUniverse books may be ordered through booksellers or by contacting:

iUniverse
1663 Liberty Drive
Bloomington, IN 47403
www.iuniverse.com
1-800-Authors (1-800-288-4677)

ISBN: 978-1-4620-4208-1 (sc)
ISBN: 978-1-4620-4210-4 (hc)
ISBN: 978-1-4620-4209-8 (ebk)

Printed in the United States of America

iUniverse rev. date: 08/17/2011

Orphan Child

Loved by some, hated by many . . .
but respected by all . . . O

CHAPTER 1

"Jermel sit your ass down!" screamed Betty.

Betty was a single mother trying to get her life back on track. She had recently come home from a Women's Federal Prison in Danbury, Connecticut. She was given 72 months for Aiding, Abetting, and Robbery. She was caught driving the getaway car after a ten block high speed chase that ended with a crashed car, her broken collar bone, and the death of her boyfriend Chico, who was the brain behind their capers.

During the last year of her incarceration she met a guy named Al, short for Alvin, through one of their close friends she had been robbing with. Betty and Al starting writing one another often, and boy did Al have a way with words! He was also locked up and expecting to come home soon. He was the type of guy that had done a lot of reading and came off as very intelligent, but was slick and conniving. He was able to hold her attention for the remainder of her stay. They both were released around the same time, and the bond that they had brought them close ending in a solid union. Betty soon became pregnant and was happily looking forward to the birth of their first child.

Four months into the pregnancy Al started disappearing for days at a time. He was up to his old tricks again, and Betty had no idea what was going on. What she didn't know was that Al liked that 'blow'. The power and rush that the powder would give him when it hit his nose was like nothing else. It became his main priority in which nothing came before and nothing else mattered.

Al had the gift of gab and started using it to swindle people he knew and people he met for cash and whatever else he could get. Before long, he was going hard robbing any and everything in sight for the drug that had once again taken over his life.

Betty soon realized his addiction his addiction and put his sorry ass out. She didn't need a dope fiend around her newborn baby. By the time she had Jermel she was able to move on without him, and Al was no place to be found. After she had her baby, she got a good job at a group home on 14th and Shepherd St. where she was a counselor for young girls who had either been abandoned by their parents or abused in some type of way.

Betty got along good with most all the kids because she could relate to what they were going through so well. She grew up in one of the meanest hoods in Washington, D.C., known by all as Valley Green. It was known for murder and mayhem back in those days . . . this was also where she was abandoned as a child.

Betty was also loved by Mrs. Johnston who worked there. Mrs. Johnston had been there for over twenty years and was looked at as the grandmother to all the girls who lived there. She would keep the peace, and was always the one who stepped in when things started to get out of hand in the home.

Jermel loved Grandma Johnston and showed off whenever they were around one another. Knowing that she wouldn't let him get his ass whooped by his mother Betty, he would often show out even more. Mrs. Johnston went by the name "Mother" throughout the house and by all the girls, including Betty. "Mother," said Betty, "If anything was to ever happen to me, would you please take care of Jermel for me?" "Girl ain't anything ever going to happen to you, but if it did, then yes Jermel will always have a home with me." "That's good to know," said Betty with a big smile upon her face. She only wanted the best for her son, and found comfort in knowing that Mrs. Johnston agreed to be there for him after raising six kids of her own. All of them are now grown but she still lives in the four bedroom row house on 9th and Upsher St. on the Northwest side of town where she raised them.

After about a year of working together, Betty and Mrs. Johnston had formed a close relationship, like mother and daughter. Not only did they work together, they often spent time together on their days off. The most common interest that they both shared was bingo. They both loved it! Every Wednesday and Saturday night if they did not have to work, they were at bingo faithfully whether they got there in rain, sleet, or snow.

Jermel woke up from taking a nap and got up to see what his mom was doing. He jumped up on the bed Betty had been sleeping in and she awoke in a rage. "Boy didn't I tell your bad ass about waking me up! Get up here and lay your butt down beside me." As he proceeded to lie down beside her, Betty yelled for her friend La Quita to wake her up at 3:00 pm for work. La Quita had been staying with her to keep her company since Al wasn't there anymore. On top of that, she was working quite a bit and needed help with Jermel.

"Okay," replied La Quita as she went back into the living room. She then curled up on the couch and began to apply nail polish to her toes. It took her a little over an hour to redo her nails and toes. La Quita looked at the clock. "Damn it's 3:05," she said to herself. "Let me go wake this girl up before she be cursing me out."

As she walked to Betty's room she called out for her. "Betty," she called, waking Jermel up instead. She got to Betty and shook her to wake up, but she was not responding. Getting hysterical because her friend was not waking up, she ran to dial 911. "911, what is your emergency?" asked the dispatcher at the other end of the line. "Yes," said La Quita frantically, "my friend was sleeping and I was supposed to wake her up at 3 pm for work but she won't wake up! I shook her and she's not responding!" The dispatcher replied calmly, "Miss, first of all you have to calm down so that I can get the information that I need to help you."

"Okay", said La Quita on the verge of crying.

"Have you checked her pulse Miss?" asked the dispatcher. "Look bitch, get the fucking ambulance over her right now and stop asking so many dumb questions!" La Quita snapped. She then dropped the phone to pick up Jermel who was now scared and crying, grabbing her around her legs.

The ambulance arrived about ten minutes later and two paramedics rushed into the apartment. After a few tests La Quita could sense that things were not good. After a few more repeated attempts to revive her, they put her on the stretcher and rushed her to Georgetown University Hospital with La Quita and Jermel riding along.

After about an hour at the hospital a doctor came out to the waiting room and asked if there was anyone there for Betty Cherry. "Yes, I am," replied La Quita as she hurried to the doctor with Jermel in tow. "Miss," the doctor said quietly gently touching her shoulder and looking her genuinely in the eye, "I'm sorry, but we were not able to bring her back." The short curly haired doctor who could easily pass for Arabic descent went on, "We have done everything that we can but she passed away from cardiac arrest."

La Quita began to cry uncontrollably. She could not believe she had just lost her friend, who was only twenty seven years old, from a heart attack. In her mind, tragedies like these were not supposed to happen. As she wept, Jermel began to cry as well although he did not yet know why. At this point he just wanted his mom.

CHAPTER 2

<u>TEN YEARS LATER</u>

"Grandma, can Jermel and I go to the rec and play some basketball?" asked John-John. "Go ahead, but make sure you watch them cars when you cross the streets," Mrs. Johnston answered.

Jermel was now 11 years old. Mrs. Johnston had raised him since he was almost two, just after Betty passed. Mrs. Johnston did not mind taking him in at all. In fact, she was very happy since she was starting to get lonely in her old age and needed a new challenge in her life. Besides that, she had already grown to love him immensely and wanted to give him the best life he could have.

Mrs. Johnston already had a big family. All six of her children had their own kids, some older than Jermel and some around the same age and a few were younger than him. Mrs. Johnston was a very strong woman. She was the glue that held her family together and demanded that they stick together at all times. Loyalty was a must amongst one another.

Her oldest son Big John was the worst of them all. He made his living in the streets and was known for robbing and being a trickster. He was the type that would rob and kill his best friend if there was enough money involved. He always said that there was only one rule when you were in the streets, and that was to get money. He taught the younger ones in the family to always have each other back and fuck everybody else.

He said to always remember that blood is thicker than water. Big John always drove the best cars and wore nothing but top of the line suits and gators. He also had his way with women. All of his kids were by a different woman.

Jermel, just as his sons and nephews, looked up to Big John as a legend. All they saw was the fame and glitter, and wanted to be just like him. Most of the male family members under him looked at Big John like Jermel did and had patterned their life in his footsteps. They started off selling drugs on the corner, and went on capers when the opportunities came available. Everyone in the neighborhood knew that the Johnston family was strong, and if you fucked with one then be prepared to deal with the consequences.

Jermel soon realized the muscle of the Johnston's and wanted to prove himself as part of the family. Although he did not have their blood in his veins, he knew that he could go just as hard as they did. Jermel was a little before his time and at the age of twelve had gotten his first gun, a .380 caliber pistol.

"Man hurry up and bag that shit up," said Big John. "You know them dope fiends is going to be out there trying to get their fix by 6:30 this morning."

"I got this," Beanie sighed.

"I told you last night we had to get this shit done when you was fucking wit that freak ass bitch Precious," Big John said.

"I'm going to clean this shit up and I'll be right out," said Beanie.

As Big John walked to the car he was driving, he noticed a white Nissan Maxima parked at the end of the block with three men with dread locks sitting inside. That was unusual for the neighborhood they were in. Big John played it cool and kept walking as though he was not on point. The Maxima pulled slowly from its parking spot and proceeded in his direction.

Big John positioned himself close to the car he was driving and pulled his nine from his waistline while making it look like he was putting the key in the door. He eyed the strange car closely as it moved closer. One of the occupants attempted to put a Mac-Nine out of the window, but Big John beat him to the punch letting his nine spray bullets in the direction of the car. Slugs slammed into the front and driver side of the car striking the driver in the face and chest, killing him instantly. The other two men hopped out of the car shooting continuously in Big John's direction causing him to retreat behind a car. He was no match for the two gunmen that would take him out any second.

"Damn this might be the end!" thought Big John as he ducked behind the car, knowing he was out of bullets to fight back. Suddenly he heard a hail of bullets slicing through the air. Big John braced himself anticipating the lava hot burn of bullets ripping into his flesh. The popping sounds stopped and moments later he seen Beanie standing over him with an Uzi in his hand.

"Come on! We got to get the fuck out of here!" exclaimed Beanie.

"Yeah let's go!" said Big John, leaving behind three dead men with dreadlocks.

"That was them Jamaicans from around 14th and Girard St. that we took the weed from," said Beanie.

"I wonder how the fuck they know where we be staying at," said Big John. "That was a close call; them motherfuckers almost had my ass."

"I'm hip," replied Beanie. "Good thing I didn't have that music pumping like I usually do, because I probably wouldn't have heard them gunshots."

Beanie and big John had narrowly escaped death.

Jermel had just gotten out of school at Petworth Elementary, which was only a few blocks away from where he lived.

"Jermel let's stop at the rec," said Jermel's best friend, Man.

"We can do that," said Jermel. "Alicia and them be having cheerleading practice after school."

Man said, "You scared of that broad. You always want to be around her but you never say anything to her."

"I ain't scared of shit. I just don't be sweating them hookers like you do," said Jermel.

As they approached the ninth they noticed a crowd of people standing in the street. They could tell it was a fight going on by all the shouting and ranting. Jermel and Man walked swiftly into the crowd to get a piece of the excitement. The closer Jermel got, he noticed that a lot of the people were family members. He heard his Aunt Dee Dee screaming in the crowd, "You better whip his ass or I'm going to whip yours!"

"Shawty that's your peoples," said Man.

"I see," said Jermel.

Jermel inched his way into the crowd and seen his cousin Bernard fighting the dude Manny from Seventh St. They both had a reputation for fighting and everybody knew they were going to bump heads sooner or later.

Many of Manny's people were in the crowd as well. Jermel had seen times like this in his young life when one on one fights would turn into huge family on family brawls. Jermel reached in his backpack, took out his .380 and put it in his front pocket. He had made up his mind that if this one started to get out of hand, somebody from the opposite team was going to get it!

Ring . . . . ring . . . . ring. "Hello," Big John answered his phone.

"What's up Cuz?" asked Beanie on the line.

"Man it's early as shit. What the fuck do you want?" growled Big John.

"Stop crying. I'm calling to tell you I found out Precious was the one that told them dreads where the party was at," Beanie replied.

"Oh yea?" said Big John.

"Yeah you know her little sister got a baby by one of them, so you know they got history," Beanie replied.

"Alright, good looking," said Big John as he was hanging up the phone to call Precious.

Rinnnggg . . . . ringgg . . . . "Hello," answered Precious, sounding like she had just woke up.

"What's up Baby?" asked Big John, as if he missed her. "I know it's early but I got a surprise for you. Get up and get dressed, I'll be there in an hour to get you."

"Where are we going at five in the morning?" asked Precious.

"Baby I told you it's a surprise, but our plane leaves at 8 am," Big John said.

"Okay!" replied Precious, excited.

"Alright, bye" said Big John hanging up.

Precious hung up and hurried to the shower. He was talking her language when he talked about a plane leaving. Precious was a thirty-five year old head turner. She was often mistaken for a woman in her twenties. She stood about five feet eight inches with long black hair. Her jet black hair and her frame reminded you of Stacey Dash. On top of that, she wore nothing but designer clothing and accessories. Gucci and Chanel were her favorite stores. Unless you knew her, you would think that she was wife material. She had mastered the art of deception, using her looks, pussy, and other manipulation skills she had acquired throughout life. Precious had gotten dressed and was putting on her earrings when she heard the horn blow.

She looked out the window and saw Big John's Porsche 911 waiting in front of her building. She grabbed her purse and luggage and headed for the elevator to meet Big John.

"What's up Baby?" asked Big John. "You wearing the shit out of that dress."

"Thank you", said Precious as she leaned out and gave Big John a kiss on the side of his face. "So where we going?"

"Vegas," replied Big John. "I've been planning this for us for a few weeks now. I always show my women a nice time."

"I hear you daddy," said Precious.

Big John turned up the tunes of Al Green and cruised on the highway towards Dulles Airport.

CHAPTER 3

The commotion in the street had stopped traffic. People were blowing their horns and yelling out of their windows for the crowd to disperse. An old lady was on her cell phone talking to what appeared to be the police by the way she was looking up at the street signs, as if trying to find her location.

"Man let's go. I think that old lady just called the law," Jermel told Man.

"Alright let's go over there on the field so we can still see what's going on over here," said Man.

Three police cars bolted around the corner where the disturbance was. The cops jumped out of their cars and pulled black jacks from their waist. The crowd scattered displaying a clear view of the two teenagers still slugging in the street. Two of the officers separated the two boys with excessive force, slamming them onto their backs.

"Motherfuckers don't be slamming my nephew like that!" shouted Dee Dee coming towards the officer.

"Miss, I advise you to back up before I lock your sorry ass up," replied the officer in a cocky tone.

"Fuck that! And fuck you motherfucker! That's a fourteen year old boy y'all manhandling like that!" Dee Dee said angrily.

"Lock her ass up!" shouted the officer.

The Tom Cruise looking officer put cuffs on her and walked her towards the police car. Dee Dee continued to curse the officers out as she was dragged past the one that initiated the arrest. She spit in his face as she was thrown into the back seat of the cruiser. She was the fierce type that wasn't scared of anyone, male or female. Big John trained her well. She was his baby sitter and he was really over protective when it came to her.

Jermel and Man watched as the police car drove by with Bernard, and then the next car drove by with Dee Dee in the back. Jermel stared in a daze.

"Jermel, what's up?" asked Man.

"Ain't shit up, I was just thinking," answered Jermel.

"Let's go to the courts," suggested Man.

"Alright," said Jermel.

They walked to Petsworth Rec Center, which was where most of the kids often went after school. The rec always had some type of activity going on for the youngsters when school was out. As they reached the front of the Rec where the girls practiced their routines, Jermel saw Alicia chasing Lil Ty with tears in her eyes.

"You better not touch me anymore you black dog!" screamed Alicia.

As she walked back over to where the other girls were, Lil Ty ran up behind her and squeezed her ass with both hands while laughing as if it was the funniest thing in the world. Alicia saw a beer bottle on the ground, picked it up and whipped it at his head. He saw what was happening just in time to duck and hear the bottle shatter on the wall behind him.

"That's right! You better duck!" said Alicia.

"Bitch if that bottle would have hit me I would have fucked your ass up!" shouted Lil Ty.

"Motherfucker you ain't going to fuck nobody up!" Jermel said as he stepped in front of Lil Ty.

"Jermel you better get the fuck out my face. You don't have shit to do with this," replied Lil Ty.

"Fuck you," said Jermel.

"No, fuck your mother." answered Lil Ty.

"Remember you said that you bitch ass nigga," said Jermel.

Mr. Green, who was working in the rec came jogging out of the building and defused the argument. Jermel was pissed. He couldn't stand when someone said something about his mother.

"Jermel, don't worry about him. He ain't trying to do nothing," said Man.

"Man leave me alone," replied Jermel.

Man looked at him, "What you getting mad at me for? I didn't do nothing to you."

"I never said you did, did I?" snapped Jermel.

"Alright champ, I'm gone then," said Man.

Jermel didn't say anything. He just stood and watched every move Lil Ty made. Nonchalantly Lil Ty went on his way into the rec center to play ping pong before going to the basketball court and called next.

Jermel was just sitting there on the bench with his backpack when Alicia walked over to him.

"Jermel thank you so much for taking up for me."

"That's what I was supposed to do," said Jermel.

"Alright, bye Jermel, I'll see you tomorrow at school," Alicia said, smiling as she turned to walk away.

"Alright," replied Jermel as he watched her look over her shoulder to smile at him.

It was about 6:30pm as Jermel continued to watch Lil Ty get his coat and hat off the fence. He knew Lil Ty was about to go home, and Jermel knew which way he had to go to get there. He watched as Lil Ty walked down the steps and onto 7th St. Jermel quickly ran across the grass of the rec and into the alley which led to 8th St. He knew that Lil Ty had to come past the alley to get to his house. Out of breath, Jermel took off his backpack to retrieve his .380. He looked up to see if his target was coming and saw Lil Ty turning the corner onto the other side of the street from where Jermel was in the alley.

Jermel's heart was racing, adrenaline pumping through his veins. He had been carrying that gun around every day since he had gotten it. Today he was going to prove to himself that he would use it. His hands were sweaty and unsteady as he cocked the pistol and made his move from the alley into the street firing the silver .380 recklessly. The small gun bucked in his hands as bullets ricocheted off cars as Lil Ty dropped his books and ran in the other direction in a flash.

Jermel had blacked out firing all six of the bullets he had in his gun. He heard the click of the trigger and realized he was out of ammunition. Slowly the sounds of the environment around him came into focus. He heard the screams of the innocent bystanders who had taken cover on the ground behind the cars and a random dog barking in the distance. Jermel realized he was just standing there holding the pistol in the open and realized he had to get out of there.

Jermel ran back into the alley, put the gun in his bag, and took off through the dark. After a few shortcuts he was soon at the corner of Upsher St. where he lived. He gathered his composure and walked up the block calmly as if he hadn't done a thing. He got to his house, went in the front door, and directly to his room where he sat and thought. The more he thought, the more he felt like a warrior. The power of the gun had amazed him. The feeling of the recoil going through his arm, the flash from the end of the barrel, and his enemy running from him overwhelmed him. He laid in his bed and replayed the events of the day over and over in his head, enjoying it more and more each time. He vowed to himself that the next time he shot at Lil Ty he would not miss. What he said about Jermel's mother would be avenged.

CHAPTER 4

"Please put your seat belts on and prepare for landing. We will be landing in Las Vegas in approximately ten minutes", the pilot crackled through the speakers on the plane.

"Baby wake up," Precious said. "The stewardess is coming around to make sure all seat belts are secure."

"Damn we here already?" asked Big John.

"You've been asleep ever since we got on the plane," Precious answered.

"I know, I was fucking tired," said Big John stretching.

"When we get to the room I'm going to give you a massage and run you a hot bubble bath," Precious said in her best seductive voice.

They both sat up in their seats as the plane skipped on the runway in its first attempt to stop. Finally stopping, the plane taxied to the gate after a few more minutes. Big John and Precious exited the plane in a hurry trying to beat the crowd. Big John went straight to the concession stand and ordered a double shot of Remy.

"Baby come on, the cab driver is waiting for us," said Precious. "Our bags are already in the car."

"I'm coming," replied Big John. "I just needed a drink to wake me up."

Big John told the cab driver to take them to the Four Caesars Casino Resort. While riding to the hotel, Big John put his arms around Precious pulling her close to him and letting her head rest on his chest. They watched the bright lights of Vegas as the cab drove down the strip towards their destination. Shortly afterwards, the driver pulled in front of the hotel door. They got out and walked towards the glass and gold doors as the bell hop took their luggage. Precious smiled at the luxury of their accommodations.

While on the plane Big John told Precious to use the air phone to call and make reservations for the best suite that The Four Caesars had to offer. When they checked in, their room was a penthouse on the top floor.

Big John tipped the bell hop with a big faced bill and told him to take their luggage up to the suite. From there they went straight to the casino floor. "Here you go," said big John handing her a big stack of bills, "that should hold you for awhile."

"Thank you baby," said Precious smiling. "I'm about to go to the Black Jack table, I feel like today might be my lucky day!"

"It sure is bitch," Big John thought to himself.

They walked in the direction of the Black Jack tables before being stopped by a beautiful waitress who offered drinks. That was the hospitality of the hotel. The girls looked as if they should be runway models, but instead made more money off tips from serving alcohol to high rollers. They always treated their big spenders the best.

"Black Jack!" said Precious as the dealer flipped over the Jack of Spades to match the Ace that was showing in front of her. Big John ordered two bottles of Dom Perion Champagne as he watched Precious enjoy the last good time she'd ever have.

After two hours at the table and several glasses of champagne, Precious had won over five thousand dollars. She always placed large bets when she gambled. It seemed that indeed it was her lucky day and she was winning big.

"Let's go up to the room," said Precious.

"That sounds like a great idea," replied Big John.

"I know right, before my luck changes," she said. "I want to go get in the shower and change."

"I feel you, it's been a long day," answered Big John.

Precious and Big John entered the elevator and went upstairs to the penthouse. It was registered in Precious name but paid for with Big John's cash. When he told her to check them in and gave her a stack of cash to pay for it, she thought nothing of it since he had mentioned something about not having his ID with him. She didn't care, all she saw was green.

As the door opened to their room Precious gasped in awe. The marble floors and the view from the balcony and the hot tub that displayed the beautiful overlook of Downtown Vegas aroused her.

The air was cool as they stepped out on the balcony. When they looked down, the traffic below was moving as if it were rush hour.

"Baby this place is so perfect," said Precious walking back into the room admiring the luscious couch made with the best Italian leather. Big John made his way over to the sofa beside Precious with the two glasses of Remy he had just poured at the bar. "Let's toast," he said. "This is to having a good time together."

"Baby we always have a good time together," said Precious, raising her glass in the air to meet his. "I'm going to the bathroom to freshen up."

"Don't have me waiting too long," sighed Big John. His charm had her blushing like a little school girl as she got up and made her way to the bathroom.

"That bitch got a mean fucking walk," thought Big John as he moved to turn up the sounds of the Isley Brothers' 'In Between the Sheets'. He pulled a hundred dollar bill out of his wallet that had been folded a couple times and rolled it up. After rolling the bill, he poured a small amount of dope onto the granite counter of the bar and cut it up into three lines. After the toots, he poured himself another drink and walked out on the balcony to get some fresh air.

Precious came out of the bathroom wearing a black satin robe, displaying clearly that she had nothing on under it. Her silky long hair was still wet from the shower making her look sexier than ever. She slowly walked out to where Big John was and put her arms around his waist. She rubbed his chest and stomach before loosening his belt and pants. Positioning herself in front of him, she stroked his manhood while passionately licking his neck. She kneeled and started to slowly lick up and down the side of his pride and joy, teasing him by sliding her tongue around the head in small circles. Big John leaned back on the railing in ecstasy. Precious knew that she was fulfilling him by the way he bit on his bottom lip. She was a pro at seduction and she knew it. When she sensed that he was getting too aroused, she stopped, dropped her robe and walked back in towards the bedroom with her ass shaking every step of the way. Big John followed, taking off his clothes as he walked behind her.

Precious started thinking to herself, "If this motherfucker is going to be spending money like this, I have to give him special treatment!" She laid on her back with her legs spread, welcoming him into her world. He climbed over her and licked her breast, gently sucking one nipple then the other. He made love trails from her nipples slowly up to her earlobe.

Precious was getting hot from the foreplay. Moaning, she whispered for him to enter her. He then made his way to her navel where he planted soft kisses before reaching her wetness that was perfectly shaved for his convenience. He licked around the edges in a slow motion making her squirm as he worked his magic. It wasn't long before he was gently sucking and pulling on her clitoris, driving her to the peak of ecstasy.

Big John turned her over and told her to put the pillow under her stomach as he entered her doggy style. He dug aggressively into her as she held on to the sheet in total submission. The lovemaking went on for hours before Big John went into the living room to take another blow.

Precious woke up an hour later and saw that Big John was in the other room so she went to see what he was doing. "What's up baby?" she asked, taking a seat beside him wearing nothing but bra and panties.

"Ain't shit. I'm just enjoying being stress free for a change. I'm about to make me a drink, do you want one?" he asked her.

"Yeah babe, I'll take one," she replied.

"Precious do me a favor and get my wallet out of my pants for me while I make our drinks," Big John told her.

"Okay, I'll be right back."

As Precious went to get the wallet he poured two shots of Remy. In one of the glasses, he dropped four drops of Visine. Relaxing, he sat the glasses on the table and waited for her to return.

"This is for the best sex ever," said Big John as he picked up his glass.

"I'll drink to that!" shouted Precious, picking up her glass and swallowing the liquor in one gulp.

They continued drinking until she went out for the count. He had used the old Visine method on her that he use to use on them broads that use to fake with the pussy. A few drops of Visine in their drinks and they'd be yours for the night.

Once she was out he dragged her to the bathroom and sat her on the floor. He got out the syringe and the pure black tar heroin that he'd gotten from one of the local drug buys while she was playing Black Jack. He drew up 100 units of water and put it in a spoon and began to cook it by holding it over the flame from his lighter. Once the water became a dark brown color, he took the cotton, put it on the end of the needle and drew the thick liquid into the syringe. Putting the syringe into her arm, he drew the plunger back until it pulled in her blood to make sure that it was right in her vein. He hit her with the dope, waited about twenty seconds and checked her pulse. It was still beating, but slowly. He repeated the process, and realized as he was checking it this time that she had stopped breathing. She was gone.

Precious laid lifeless on the bathroom floor with the needle still in her arm as Big John stepped over her and closed the bathroom door behind him. He grabbed all his things and went down the stairs, leaving the five thousand she had won in her bag. Housekeeping would find her in the morning and call the police. The police would figure just another accidental overdose from partying hard, one of thousands of accidents that happened each year in Vegas. Big John smiled as he got in the cab to go back to the airport.

CHAPTER 5

From that day on Jermel felt like he would always be in control of his world as long as he had a gun in his possession, so he made an oath to never leave home without it. He was still disappointed that he had missed Lil Ty and vowed that it would never happen again. He thought about Big John's saying, "If you're going to do something, do it by yourself. And if you make an attempt to do something, make sure that it's thought out and done strategically." Jermel learned a lot from watching old heads around the neighborhood. Some things he used, some things he didn't. He liked school for the most part and wanted to do well. He was also a little shy around the other kids and wouldn't talk unless asked something.

Jermel and Man had been friends since the sandbox and always had each other's back. School had just closed for the summer and Jermel turned thirteen. One day Jermel and Man decided to walk up Georgia Avenue to see what was going on. They would often walk up there to see the girls that would come from all over the city to chill, wanting one of the young hustlers to holler at them. Young hustlers were on both sides of the street, up and down the Ave. That had been one of Northwest's major drug strips since the 70's. Enticed by what they seen, they both wanted some of the action.

"Man let's go over there where that crowd of people at," said Jermel.

"Come on. I think they over there shooting craps," answered Man as they started in the crowd's direction.

They walked up to the crowd of young men and noticed everyone had stacks in their hands. "Shoot fifty," said one man standing next to Man who was wearing a black linen short set with some black Gucci loafers to match. Jermel and Man stood there and watched the men shoot craps and looked at all the money that was exchanged from one hand to another. That was the night Jermel decided that he was going to get him some money. "If they can do it, I can do it too," he thought.

Man was on the same page so they decided to hang out up there every day and try to figure out how to get some. One day one of the old heads asked them if they wanted to get some money. "Hell yeah," they both said in unison. The old head, who went by the name 'Black', gave them both twenty little bags of crack a piece. Each bag was ten dollars. They gladly accepted and told Black that they'd be back as soon as they got his money.

Over the next few days they started moving the crack and started making some money. Jermel was a natural at hustling and didn't let anyone get anything on front. If you didn't have the cash then you didn't get nothing. Man on the other hand, had a tough time learning the game and would let the fiends swindle him out of his stuff by telling him that they'd pay him later or switch bags on him when he showed it to him with slight of hand.

Black saw the potential in the youngins and took them under his wing. Black was from Park Road, a side street off of Georgia Ave. He had put his work in over the years and was well respected both in the hood and out. He drove the best cars and wore the finest clothes.

Jermel admired Black like the big brother he never had. He didn't only teach the youngsters how to survive in the street; he also taught them how to be men. Jermel and Man didn't carry themselves like the average teens. Black taught them to respect and demand respect in return. He also told them to stay in school because knowledge was the key to whatever they chose to do in life. The more you knew about something, the better you would be at doing it.

Jermel was very receptive to what Black was teaching him. He told himself that he would always stay in school and keep as many people as possible out of his business. Black had warned him that jealousy was a part of the game.

One Sunday afternoon Jermel was standing on Park Road where he was spending most of his time, when a blue Yukon drove up. Streaking to a stop beside him two men he didn't know jumped out, snatched him and threw him in the truck. Jermel fought to get away but was no match for the two oversized men. Once in the truck they immediately took his gun from out his waistline.

Jermel knew they weren't police from the strong smell of weed that polluted the air.

"Shorty where Black at?" asked the driver.

"I don't know!" answered Jermel anxiously.

"Look shorty, I fucking know he fucks with you and you know where his stash spot at. So you're going to take us to it or you're going to fucking die," shouted the other man beside him pointing a Glock 40 at him.

"I don't know what the fuck you're talking about! He didn't show me where shit at!" Jermel shouted back.

"Shorty you think we're playing with your little ass, don't you? We'll go somewhere and show you how much we're playing!" shouted the enraged driver.

Jermel didn't say anything from that point on. He was watching his surroundings carefully, trying to figure out a way to escape or drain a tip outside that he was being kidnapped. The driver drove downtown before getting on the 9th St. Tunnel.

He was taken to a neighborhood on the southside of the city. By this time, Jermel was shaken up bad. All he could think of was how they was going to kill him. He was terrified.

They pulled into some apartments and the truck stopped. Duct tape was placed over his mouth and a coat over his head. The two oversized men dragged him into one of the apartments close by. They sat him down on a couch and took the coat off his head. Jermel looked around and saw only the ratty couch he was sitting on and an old black and white TV with rabbit ears sitting on the kitchen counter.

Jermel started to cry because he knew they were going to kill him, and all he could think about was the hurt that Mrs. Johnston would experience.

"Shorty look at me . . . Look at me motherfucker!" shouted the big man standing in front of him. He held the Glock in his right hand by his side. Jermel looked up through his tears.

"I told you to tell me where the shit at. Now this is your last fucking time to tell me where it is or . . . oh well, you know what's going to happen."

The guy was calm but Jermel could see the rage in his dark eyes. He thrust the gun at Jermel and held it an inch from his forehead.

Jermel was now shaking and crying uncontrollably as he spoke through his tears. "I told you man, he never took me over there."

The interrogation lasted a couple more minutes before Black walked out the back room. Jermel saw him but wasn't sure what was happening.

"Jermel calm down," Black said to him.

It was at that moment Jermel realized what was happening. It had been a test. He was both relieved and pissed at the same time. He realized that every man in the room had at some point taken and passed that same test. Black was on loyalty hard, and even though he took a liking to Jermel he still would have killed him if he hadn't passed that test.

Black looked at Jermel. "Ain't nothing personal shorty. It's just better to know for sure what people would do when death was on the table than to guess."

Jermel was still upset and a bit mad at Black for questioning his integrity, but he understood. The experience made Jermel realize just how real shit was when playing this type of game.

"Look Mel, I'm about to start giving you thousand dollar packs for six hundred. Think you can handle that?" Black asked him.

"I don't see why not," replied Jermel.

"Black tossed him the bag and said, "Good, you start now."

Jermel was happy but didn't stop to the math before accepting the deal. The packs that Black was giving him now would only make him five hundred dollars more per hundred than he was making before.

All Jermel thought about was how he was going to be the flyest one in school when it started back. This year he was going to start junior high so he had to have his gear together. It had been a few weeks since the arrangement with Black and he was grinding hard. He had saved about three thousand dollars and in his eyes he was on his way to being rich.

Jermel and Man were standing on the block after getting rid of their last little bit of work, when Big John pulled up and told them to get in.

"What's up OG?" asked Man.

"Ain't shit really," replied Big John. "I just want yall to take a ride with me."

"Alright," they both answered.

"Look, I want to talk to y'all about something," Big John said as he pulled onto the street. "I heard y'all been out here slingin stones for that nigga Black. I already talked to him and told him not to give y'all shit else. I thought I taught you better than that."

Jermel just listened trying to figure out where he was going with this.

"How long has he been giving you that shit?" he asked.

"Shit, I dunno. Four, maybe five weeks," Man answered.

"And how much money do you think y'all made him?" Big John wanted to know.

"Between the two of us, probably like ten thousand dollars," they both agreed.

"I saved up almost three thousand!" said Jermel enthusiastically feeling proud of himself.

"You got under three thousand and you made over ten? It never registered in your big ass head that something was seriously wrong with that picture?" Big John asked. "You never let nobody pimp you like that! You ain't no slave. If you're going to be fucking with that shit then you sell that shit for yourself. Build your own empire. Make yourself rich."

Big John looked over at Jermel. "You see what I'm saying now?"

"Yeah, you're right," said Jermel with a slight nod, "I see what you're saying."

Jermel had learned another lesson from Big John and felt stupid for being used like that. After Big John laying down the law for them, he took them to get something to eat then took them home. They didn't quit fucking with Black though; they just started buying as much weight as they could afford and bagged it themselves instead of getting fronted packages.

Black didn't know that Jermel was Big John's people. He respected Big John so the fact that he was looking out for them worked well and he gave the youngins good deals. Jermel and Man quickly noticed the difference from selling Black's shit to selling their own product. They saw a much larger profit and didn't need to answer to anyone but themselves. They could never get ahead like they wanted to though because everytime they finished selling, they'd go shopping, leaving them with just enough money to re-up. They were happy though.

By the time school started back they had all the latest attire and stood out in school as money getters. All the girls that wouldn't speak to them in the past now went out of their way to acknowledge them. The dudes started to get jealous of them because of their money and fame with the girls. This was a lot different than elementary school Jermel thought as he walked the halls going to his class. He had made up his mind. If anybody jumped out there with him, then he would deal with them.

Over the summer Jermel bought every gun that he could get his hands on. His theory concerning guns was 'the more, the better'. He kept it to himself and the only person that knew what he carried was Man. Jermel now carried a Sig Sauer 9mm Automatic, but also had bigger guns such as his Colt 1911 .45 and a Desert Eagle .50. The Sig was comfortable to carry and the blue steel of the gun was comforting to have in his possession. It made him happier every time he looked at it. All the dudes at school had guns, but most of those were piece of shit .22 revolvers or old .38's. There were shootings and murders all around him on the regular at this stage of life, so he felt safer knowing that he had the best arsenal of anyone he knew.

Jermel now hung out and hustled on 7th and Taylor St. and Lil Ty hung out on 13th and Shepherd St., Lil Ty never forgot about Jermel trying to kill him so Jermel knew he couldn't sleep on him since Lil Ty had heard about the work that he had been putting in. Lil Ty was Jermel's first enemy. He knew that he had to apply everything he learned to survive in the streets.

One day after school Jermel and Man decided to make an early start on the block. Jermel felt like he was been seen more when he left out during the day and started disguising himself with hats and hooded sweatshirts while he was on the block. He understood that when you were living in the streets you have to be careful as possible. Another thing that he's learned was to never make yourself an easy target for the two forces that haunted you the most out there. Those were the law and the other, your enemies.

Jermel said to himself that he would always be a moving target. This particular day happened to be on the first of the month. This was the day that most money getters made exceptions to their regular routines due to the greed they had for the little green promissory notes they saw as wealth. The first through the third were the days that the Department of Treasury issued checks to the recipients that qualify for the government ran welfare program.

7th and Taylor St., like most neighborhoods in the D.C. area had a lot of addicts that got assistance from the government but would spend their checks with the first street hustler that had the product of their choice.

Jermel and Man were amongst the greedy hustlers. They had grown an obsession with money but had a terrible spending habit. They always had to have new clothes and shoes, keeping up with the latest trends.

When they arrived on the block it was just as they had expected. It was alive with a lot of activity just like the first of every other month. There were about ten other street soldiers out trying to get a piece of the action. They were positioned in different areas along the block, so Jermel and Man decided to post at the end of the alley.

Even though they knew all the people out there, they only trusted a couple of them. There had recently been robberies and murders that had obviously been inside jobs, so Jermel and Man had to be careful not to let that happen to them.

Pig and Young World was a couple of the guys out there that was alright with them. They were walking by the alley where Jermel and Man were standing and stopped to see what was up.

"What's up Mel?" asked Young World.

"Ain't shit, World. What's up with you?" Jermel answered.

"I'm just trying to take advantage of this rush," said Young World, looking around the street. "It's pumpin out her. I been out here since 12 this afternoon, but I'm about to leave as soon as I smoke these last two blunts," he said pulling out the blunts. "I don't want to leave here with any drugs on me."

"Did the police jump out around here today?" asked Man.

"They rode through a couple times but they didn't get out and search nobody," answered Pig.

"Fire that shit up!" shouted Jermel.

"C'mon. Let's go over there and sit down and smoke this shit, "agreed Young World.

They all sat on the bumper of an old Chevy Caprice Classic that was always parked on the street with a flat tire on the back driver side. The city had put a boot on the front passenger side for the numerous traffic infractions that its owner never bothered to pay. Young World lit the first stick of weed, inhaled deeply, and passed it onto Jermel. They were feeling good but waited patiently for the next one to be lit knowing it would put them exactly where they needed to be.

As Pig passed the next jay around, Jermel watched a blue Dodge Voyager minivan roll slowly in their direction. Suddenly the van accelerated towards them and slid to a stop about 40 feet away. The door to the van slid open faster than anyone could realize what was going on. The driver and the two shooters in the back swung their arms out and began firing a volley of bullets toward the four teenagers. Bullets slammed into the Caprice, shredding the other tires and shattering glass.

Jermel slid off the other side of the car and took off running as fast as he could. He heard shouting, shooting, and commotion behind him and hoped that his friends were behind him.

The episode only lasted a couple of minutes, but seemed like hours. After the sounds of the semi-automatic weapons ceased they heard the tires screech on the van as it raced away from the scene.

Jermel stopped running to see Pig and Young World close by. "Where Man at?!" he screamed frantically. The other two looked bewildered and Pig said, "I don't know. As soon as I heard the guns I started running." Young World agreed with his friend.

Jermel heard them speaking somewhere in the back of his mind as he streaked off to find Man and see if he was alright. He tried to think of excuses that maybe Man had run in a different direction and was fine, but was scared that he had been hit.

He ran back to the place he called his hood and saw Man laying in front of the Caprice. He could see the tire tracks and sun reflecting off the brass shell casings where the van had been. He looked back down at his friend and realized he was lying in a pool of blood. Things were moving in slow motion again as he looked around and saw people come out of their houses to look at the scene. He knelt down by his friend to try to see if he was still breathing. Man was staring up at him with the half blunt still hot between his fingers. He put his hands around Man's head to try to bring him back and felt his fingers sink into the soft flesh in the back of Man's head where his skull should have been. It was at that moment that he realized the red hole with a small stream of blood on the top left of his forehead. The hollow point round he had been hit with obliterated the back of his head. He stood up and looked down at his friend again and noticed the red marks in his chest and stomach. The unknown gunmen had shot his best friend three times.

As Jermel stood there he felt the tears running down his face. He looked down and saw his right hand covered with blood. He could smell death in the air and heard the police sirens approaching in the distance. His best friend had just been murdered and he did not understand why.

CHAPTER 6

With Man gone Jermel felt like a piece of him was missing. Man had lived three doors down from him on Upsher St. since he was old enough to have memories. All Jermel had thought about was how close they had been throughout their lives, how they would stay over each other's house playing Mario Brothers until the wee hours of the morning, and how they stuck together even if the odds were against them. Man was like the brother he never had. He was the only one of his friends that knew about his past. Everyone else thought that Jermel was really a part of the Johnston family. They didn't know that he was only a part of it through adoption. It was Man that he confided in when he was feeling all the neglect he could feel from being adopted.

Even though Mrs. Johnston loved Jermel with all her heart she would always refer to him as her adopted child when introducing him to her friends, leaving him feel like an outsider. Mrs. Johnston was really getting up in age and between raising six children, assisting with ten grandchildren, and twenty years spent working in child services she didn't have the energy to give Jermel the love and attention that it took to help him with all the mishaps of life.

Mrs. Johnston would work long hours. In fact, sometimes she would work for two or three days straight. Jermel knew that she had his best interest at heart but she could never show him the same motherly love that his mom would have. This caused him to have resentment toward all the bad events that occurred in his life. He often wondered why his life had to be so different from the other kids. He hated the fact that his biological parents weren't around to be a part of his life. He felt like life was against him at all times and would ask himself if there was a God that was supposed to love him, then why is he causing him so much pain in his life.

Since Jermel had been four years old, Man and he had been best friends. Man didn't have any brothers or sisters either and this allowed them to bond quickly and become inseparable. Man's mother Romaine had also looked after Jermel and cared for him as her own. She was about seventeen when she got pregnant with Man. About six months before her high school graduation.

Romaine had been an A student in school and was a good prospect to be valedictorian of her class. She had dreams of going to Harvard Law and becoming a partner at a law firm in New York City. Those dreams were shattered with her pregnancy. Although she didn't have the time anymore that was required for her to become a lawyer having to take care of Man, she was still determined to be something in life; if it not for herself, then for her baby. She had a natural talent for doing women's hair and went to cosmetology school. She had always done her friends' hair before they went out as she was growing up, and was always told that she was better than the girls that worked at the salon.

After working for numerous shops, she saved up her money and opened her own. The clients she had at the other shops that she'd worked for stayed with her, so with her talent and word of mouth, her salon went on to be one of the biggest competitors of its kind. This entrepreneur move made Romaine very successful in the process.

Man had everything he needed in life except a father. When Romaine got pregnant Man's father, P.J. denied that the baby was his. She knew he was lying because he'd been the only man that she had ever been with.

P.J. knew that there was a good possibility that he was the father, but he wasn't ready to take on responsibility. He never did want the responsibility because he never came back.

After she had Man, she never got into a serious relationship because she didn't want men in and out of his life. She dated from time to time but lived by the rule of not bringing them around Man because she didn't want him to be confused or think his mother was promiscuous.

The night of the shooting, a tall homicide detective along with his partner knocked on Man's door. Romaine had just gotten home from a long day at work. The knocks on the door irritated her because they didn't use the doorbell. She answered the door with an attitude which seemed rude to the lawmen.

"Yeah, what do you want?" shouted Romaine.

"Ma'am, are you the mother of Kenneth Hines?" asked the tall detective. "I am Detective Thomas and this is Detective Jones."

"Yeah I'm his mother. What did his bad ass do now?" She asked with a hint of irritation turning to anxiety.

"Miss Hines do you think that we can have a minute of your time to talk to you?" asked Detective Thomas.

"Sure," she answered, opening the door for them to come in. She escorted them to the living room with a worried look on her face.

"Miss Hines I am very sorry to be the one to tell you this, but Kenneth was involved in a shooting tonight and he did not make it," said Detective Jones.

Romaine began to weep and fell to the floor crying and sobbing uncontrollably. She could not believe it. This had to be some type of mistake.

"Miss Hines, I'm very sorry for your loss but I will also have to ask you to come down to the morgue to identify the body," he asked apologetically as he put his arm around her in a failed attempt to console her.

At this moment Jermel and Big John walked through. When Jermel realized what was going on and saw Romaine the way she was caused tears to roll out of his eyes. He went over to her, pushing the Detective out of the way and hugged her with specks of blood still on his shirt. That was how close he was sitting next to Man when the shots rang out.

Big John informed the detective that he was going to make sure she was alright and assured them that he would bring her to the morgue to identify the body. The detectives told him that they would be getting back with her as the details unfolded and left a card in case if she had any questions.

The rain poured as Jermel left the house to get in the car with Romaine. They were on their way to Man's funeral ceremony. Jermel had given Romaine money towards the funeral to help in a helpless situation. The ride was silent as Jermel stared out the window. He still could not truly believe this was happening.

They pulled up in front of Steward Funeral Services on Pennsylvania Ave. and were met at the car and ushered to the section of seats in the first row that was reserved for Man's immediate family. The chapel quickly filled with his family and friends from the neighborhood who all wore shirts with Man's picture on them that said 'We will always miss you!'

Man was just only fifteen and had lived a very short life. The pastor came to the podium after a series of songs and poems. By family and friends and gave a sermon aiming towards the youth that attended the service about street violence. The pastor's words made a lot of sense to Jermel and he knew that the preacher was making good points but a part of him was saying to let this be a learning experience and to leave the streets alone because it was going to end up bringing more misery than enjoyment. Another part of him was saying that he was already in too deep though. His love and loyalty for Man would not let this go unanswered.

Seeing Man lay in his casket brought a new reality to him. Jermel remembered the blood on his shirt that day and understood how easily it could have been him in that casket instead of Man. A part of him wished it was.

The last words the pastor said before leaving the podium was "start living for God and stop dying for the street."

The later it got in the service, the more difficult it got for Romaine. She knew when it was over she would never get to see her son again. The thoughts of it tore her heart apart. Dying out of order was the most terrible thing she could imagine happening. She loved her son more than herself and now would never get to see him again. She was losing all control as reality hit her.

During the viewing of the body she completely lost it. She grabbed the casket and tried to hug Man as his body lay there lifeless. The room fell silent except for the weeping of Romaine and others. Jermel, along with other family members went to her side to get her under control. Her reaction caused the other members to release their emotions as well. Most all the people in the room had tears streaming down their cheeks.

She eventually retreated into herself and Jermel was able to walk her to the stretched black Lincoln Town Car that was parked in front of the building that had been rented to take the family to the cemetery.

They got in the back of the limo and waited for Man's body to be loaded into the hearse that was parked in front of them. After the burial of Man, Jermel and the other family members went back to Romaine's house for comforting and dinner.

Big John showed up over there a short time later. He was using Man's death as a way to get closer to Romaine although Man was a loss to him. Jermel found it suspicious that he was doing this and thought it despicable. Big John was always attracted to her and flirted with her on the regular. He thought by showing his compassion it would bring him closer to her.

He came through the door with flowers and gave her a big hug. He told her that Man would want her to smile and went to the back of the house to greet the other members of the family. He saw Jermel and told him to come outside so he could talk to him. Jermel got up and followed Big John to the door that led to the back yard. Big John opened the door so that they could step out on the meticulously cared for lawn. It was so trimmed and flawless and if no one knew, they'd have thought that it was professionally maintained.

They went over to the white lawn set and sat under the large umbrella to block the sun. As Jermel took a seat he noticed a pack of Backwood Cigars that he and Man had left behind. They would always come back there to smoke trees because Romaine would kill them if she ever caught them smoking in the house.

"Jermel what's up?" asked Big John. " I know you fucked up about Man because this shit got me fucked up, too."

"I know. You don't ever expect it to really hit home," answered Jermel.

"It's fucked up, but it's part of the game," claimed Big John. "Tomorrow is not promised to you, that's why I came here to holla at you. I want you to understand this one thing. The smart survive in the street. I know you may be angry and want to kill up everything in sight, but keep in mind that there's a way to do everything. Opportunity will always present itself if you give it time and let it." He smiled, "See Jermel, real gangstas move with intelligence and not out of emotions."

"So you saying I'm in my feelings because I'm trying to find out who killed my friend?" asked Jermel angrily.

"That's not what I'm saying," Big John replied. "What I'm saying is to do your homework before you jump out there. You're not going to do Man's death no justice if you go out there and get locked up for the rest of your life or end up killed. I know how you feel shorty, I been in the streets a long time. If a lot of shit start happening in regards to this, your name is going to come up." Big John stared at Jermel to see if he understood.

"I see what you're saying," Jermel replied.

Jermel found it in him to start listening to reason. The last thing he wanted to do was catch a murder charge out of stupidity. He respected Big John and knew he wasn't going to tell him anything wrong. He realized that he did have a lot of homework ahead of him because all he really knew was that three people in a blue Dodge Voyager did a drive by on his block.

There are so many people that hang out on Taylor St. that engaged in disreputable business that there was no way to tell who the target really was. The more he thought about it, the more he decided he needed to take a step back from the block while tried to investigate what really happened.

One thing Jermel did not change his mind about from his and Big John's talk was that one way or the other he still wanted to make Man's killer pay and pay in blood. No matter who it was.

When they went back inside the house Romaine called them to the kitchen to get a plate of food she had prepared for them. Jermel got his plate off the table and saw that it had greens, potato salad, barbecue chicken wings, and dinner rolls.

"Thank you," he told Romaine, and she smiled for the first time in days.

Jermel made a vow to himself that he would always check on her and take care of her. He'd always be there if she ever needed him.

Jermel ate all the food Romaine had given him and stepped outside on the porch with the cordless phone to call Jasmine. He had been talking to her since he had been in her gym class. She won him over as soon as he saw her in the tight shorts she wore for class.

Jasmine was one of the smart, school oriented types that was very sexy without trying to be. She had a sophisticated style that stood out from the other girls in Jermel's eyes.

Jasmine knew Jermel was involved in the streets in some type of way, but he was still able to hold her attention because she was infatuated with his intellect. He would enlighten her on the history of the African culture. He had learned a lot of it from the old Moorish literature Big John had sent home from jail when he did his three year bit back in the day. He always told Jermel to learn about the true culture of his forefathers.

Jasmine was the first girl in his life that he felt that he had a real connection with. They would talk on the phone for hours at a time whenever they had a chance. They made each other happy and he missed her when he was unable to see her.

Jasmine answered the phone and asked how he was doing. He told her that he was alright that he was able to get through Man's funeral, but it had been hard. He told her how his family was there and how much he already missed Man, and about Romaine smiling when he said 'thank you' to her. He let her know that he was having dinner with Man's family and assured her that he would call her later when he left. She told him she missed him but that she understood and for him to give Romaine her condolences. She told him to make sure to call her later because she wanted to get together with him.

Jermel agreed before hanging up the phone and going back inside with everyone else.

CHAPTER 7

For Jermel, the months seemed to fly by. It seemed like just yesterday when Man and him would hang out, getting what they considered money together. Everything that Jermel did, he use to do with Man, so it was hard for him to get use to the transition.

In this era of the early 90's, Washington, DC was at its worst. It had the most murders per capital in the entire United States and was in the top five for the most violence. This was a time when the drug market was at its peak with crack, the most rapidly growing drug. Bodies were dropping left and right, either over the drug or the turf that it was being sold on. The presence of the drug had a lot of parents on the streets ignoring their children and leaving them to fend for themselves, while they were getting high and becoming addicted. If they weren't doing that, then they were probably out trying to get some of the fast cash that was being made right in their neighborhood and getting addicted to the cash in the process.

Even though there were a lot of drugs being sold, only a few reaped the benefits of the greater part of the profit. To make large profit you had to be really connected and moving a lot of weight. This cause jealously and envy to run abundant among the dealers throughout the city and made even more dangerous for them.

The streets quickly turned into a Darwinian state of survival of the fittest, where the strong became stronger and the weak became weaker. Everybody's goal was to get their piece of the money that was being made. The new hustle became capers and robberies. The stick up boys were robbing the drug boys, and the drug boys were robbing each other. Then there were the jump outs and undercover police who were taking them all.

The city was out of control and Jermel was an orphan child stuck in the middle of all the madness. He understood from a young age that he could not trust anyone except himself, and he made sure to be in control of every situation he put himself in.

It was around the sweet age of sixteen that he put his manipulation game into effect. He was looked up to by his peers for his reputation of putting in work and his arsenal of weapons. He used his street experiences and stories to intrigue the young street soldiers, subconsciously putting him on a higher plateau in their minds. His personality made him liked and disliked simultaneously.

After Man's death he didn't let any of the guys in the street get close to him. He was often looked at as aloof by those who didn't know him, because he seemed so withdrawn in himself.

Jermel didn't care how others looked at him. He lived by the motto 'Loved by some, hated by many . . . but respected by all'. He carried himself in a laid back demeanor, but never put up with anyone trying to give him a hard time.

"Jermel what's up?" asked Troy.

"Ain't shit. I'm just waiting for Jasmine to get out of class," Jermel answered, glancing at the door. "We suppose to be hanging out for a while, then going to the movies later tonight."

"That must be your girl, because you're spending a lot of time with her," Troy said.

"Well she good peoples," Jermel replied.

"You probably didn't even hit that yet," Troy said smiling.

"Ha, you got me fucked up," Jermel answered back.

"My crazy ass uncle told me that if you want to turn a broad out, you got to eat her pussy," Troy said seriously. "He said you got to get some Hall's Cough Drops."

"The fuck is that going to do?" asked Jermel.

"He said the Hall's make the pussy extra sensitive," said Troy smiling again. "I did that shit and Niecy couldn't even take it. She said it felt too fucking good."

Jermel smirked and heard the bell ringing from the school and began looking around for Jasmine.

Troy was average school guy. His brothers and cousins were heavily involved in the street and made sure that he had everything he wanted so he wouldn't turn out like them. He was very charming and had his way with the girls at school and around the neighborhood. That was one of the main reasons that Jermel had always stayed close to him, other than the fact that they had always been cool in the past anyway. Jermel knew that guys run their mouth to the girls they mess with and maybe would say something to their girl about what happened with Man. He figured that if he stayed close enough to the girls, then maybe he would find out. He was willing to use any tactic he could think of to find out what happened to his best friend and why he had been gunned down for seemingly no reason.

Jermel stood there thinking about why Man had been killed when he saw Jasmine walking towards him.

"Jermel. Jermel!" Jasmine said irritably.

Jermel started to walk in her direction. "I'm coming now."

"C'mon Jermel. You know I'm not supposed to be leaving and you down there running your mouth with your friends."

"Chill out man, I'm coming," he said to her.

They walked together through the two big brown doors that led the way out of school and to the parking lot. They moved to the left of the parking lot where Jermel had his burgundy Nissan Maxima parked. Once they got in, Jasmine finally relaxed knowing she was safe now from the school officials. She knew no one could see her behind the dark tint that Jermel had on the windows.

As Jermel started the engine, the sounds of Tupac's 'Thug Life' lightly thumped through the speakers. They drove out of the lot and off the school property into the streets. Jermel took a quick look at her while he was driving, thinking about how sexy she was. Her body reminded him of Pam on the Martin Show, which happened to be his favorite show on television. Pam was his favorite character and he found her immensely attractive.

"Baby, can you stop at the store?" Jasmine asked him breaking his train of thought.

"Alright," he responded, pulling over to the curb so she could go into the small carryout that sat on the corner of 11th and Park Road.

"I'm thirsty," said Jasmine. "I got to get me something to drink. You want me to get you anything?"

"Yeah, get me a fruit punch and a pack of Hall's Cough Drops," he told her.

"Anything else?" asked Jasmine, puzzled about the cough drops.

"Nah. That's it," Jermel answered.

As Jasmine got out of the car, her skirt rose up her leg giving him a glimpse of her thick thighs. He watched as she switched her way up to the store and got an instant hard-on when he thought that he might be getting some from her today. Although she had only had sex with him a few times, her performance was a long way from the average. She didn't like to do it often, but when she did give in he always got special treatment.

She definitely put the love spell on him and he had developed an attitude where he felt she belonged to him. He made it known to all the guys at school that she was his and they better not go near her.

Jasmine understood that he had fallen in love with her even though he never came out and told her. She could tell by his actions. She loved the way he treated her, which caused her to fall in love with him. They came from two different worlds, but they understood each other and this understanding brought them closer together.

"She better hurry up," Jermel thought to himself. He watched her through the glass in the store putting money in the turning tray so that the skinny Chinese man that owned the store could receive it through the bulletproof booth. As he watched her exit the store carrying the brown bag with the drinks and cough drops, their eyes met and she blew him a kiss. It was the loves that she gave him, that made him feel like he knew she was 'the one'.

"Where we going?" Jasmine asked him.

"I want you to meet Man's mother," Jermel replied. "She is like a mother to me and is expecting to meet you soon."

"Is that right?" Jasmine asked smiling. "You must have been talking to her about me."

"I didn't tell her nothing about you," said Jermel. "I just let her know that I have a special someone in my life, and with that she wants to meet you." Jasmine blushed and looked at Jermel, flattered by his words. They made their way to a parking space a couple of doors down from Romaine's hair salon. Jermel dumped the car by the curb and they both got out and walked up the sidewalk leading to the salon.

As they walked through the door Jermel noticed all the upgrades that had been made since the last time he had been there. There were now two beautiful women in their early twenties at their own stations repairing and airbrushing nails. Romaine also had a section at the back for men to go get their hair cut. Jermel thought it had an upscale feel to it with a touch of elegance.

All the women that worked there looked like marriage material, if looks were a determining factor.

"Jermel!" Romaine exclaimed upon seeing them walk into the salon. "Come over here and give me a hug!"

"I just wanted to stop by to see how you were doing today," he told her.

"I'm good, Sweetie," she said smiling. "This must be your friend that you are always telling me about," she said looking at Jasmine.

"My bad," said Jermel. "This is Jasmine."

"Hi Jasmine," said Romaine. "Jermel talks about you all the time. I've been around him since he was a youngster and I have never seen him this way before. You must really be something special."

"Jermel is so sweet. He brings out the best in me," Jasmine replied.

"He must bring out the worst in you too, I see he got you leaving school early," Romaine told her, still smiling. "Girl, don't look embarrassed. I'm just teasing you," Romaine laughed. "But don't get in the habit of doing that just because you like someone. School should always come first."

"You're right, and I'll keep that in mind from now on," Jasmine said, punching Jermel on the arm for getting her in trouble. She instantly gained respect for Romaine because of the words of wisdom she was just given. Jasmine admired all women of power and had dreams of patterning her life after women like Romaine who got in where they fit in with style.

Romaine stood about 5 foot 8 inches and weighed about 150 pounds. She kept her hair in a short style very similar to that of Toni Braxton. Her wardrobe mostly consisted of suits and heels. Romaine saw it as a must to always look professional because she knew that it was a good tactic for her business and it gained her much respect. Jasmine recognized this and looked up to it.

After a few more minutes with Romaine, Jermel and Jasmine left the shop and headed for the car. They both were silent in deep thought as they drove off from the spot where they parked. Every encounter with Romaine gave Jermel something new to think about. She always gave him words of wisdom to live by from a female point of view. He reminded her of the only son that she had lost to the streets. She often blamed herself for being so wrapped up in her work and not spending more time with him, instilling within him the value of life.

It was still too early for what Jermel had planned for them to do using the Hall's so he decided to stop at his house and waste some time. They were only a few blocks from his house, so it only took them a few minutes to get there. He parked his car around the corner from the house and they got out and walked.

When they arrived, Jasmine noticed the neatly planted flowers that Mrs. Johnston had planted on the sides of the walk that led to the front door. Even in her old age, Mrs. Johnston still maintained the most well kept yard on the block. When they walked through the front door they immediately noticed that the house was dark and quiet.

Jasmine could tell no one was home because Mrs. Johnston usually had the heat turned up and every light would be on in the house. Jermel smiled to himself and threw his coat on the sofa, leaving it hanging off and turned on the television to flip through different channels. Jasmine took a seat a few feet away from the couch making herself at home. Jermel kept turning the channels until he saw Mary J. and Method Man's video, 'You're all I Need' on the screen. The song reminded him so much of him and Jasmine's relationship that he loved it. Jasmine also liked the song and instantly began singing the hook along with Mary.

They sat there as B.E.T. played video after video. Jermel's teenage hormones started to play games with him as he sat beside Jasmine. His thoughts went from a humble laid back mode to a state of pure lust. He felt the process of an erection taking its course as the presence of her body lured him closer to her. Jermel moved to the love seat with her and cuddled her into his arms as they watched the TV interview with Tupac Shakur. He was talking about the recent court case in New York and of his upcoming projects in the music realm.

Jasmine had a seductive look in her eyes. Her thoughts were interrupted by voices coming from outside the front door, which is the entrance to the house. She quickly grabbed her clothes and began the struggle to put them on, feeling embarrassed at her naughty behavior. She could never face Mrs. Johnston gain if she saw her in such acts.

Jermel ran to the window to see who that could be. He knew at that time of day no one should be coming there. He looked through the corner of the blinds and noticed it was the mailman talking to the next door neighbor old man Jake.

Jermel returned and told her that it was only the mailman as she sat on the couch, who was now fully dressed and in a totally different mind frame.

Jermel came over to her and leaned down to kiss her as she turned her head away and gestured for him to have a seat beside her. She had lost all desire due to the brief interruption. It made her feel like she was doing something wrong and changed her mood.

He got the vibe and didn't press it any further, he knew how her attitude was and didn't want to make her mad. The day was early and to him he still had time to see if that halls trick really worked.

CHAPTER 8

It was a nice sunny day outside as the people in the neighborhood sat on their porches trying to enjoy as much of the last of the good weather as possible. The hood was alive with traffic from the people who came to get whichever drug they needed.

Jermel saw Pig and Young World turn the corner in Pig's 1990 blue Chevy Caprice Classic. Pig parked a few feet from where he was standing and saw water splash on his car. Every Friday he would pay a neighborhood pipehead a twenty dollar rock to wash his car. He made sure his car stayed clean, both inside and out. The inside was really a must. From past experience he knew how important it was. The city was so hot that the police would pull them over and make the boys get out, just to search for guns and drugs. They would use the complaint of smelling marijuana from their car to justify the search.

If the police really wanted to give them a hard time, they would lock them up for a couple seeds or little pieces of weed that often fell between the seats. Jermel smoked in his car on the regular, but knew that he had to cover his tracks in all aspects of the game if he was going to make it. He had to stay one step ahead of the streets and the law at all times. Riding a lot of people in his car was also against his rules since that was an open invitation for police harassment.

"What's up Jermel?" asked Young World as he walked towards Jermel.

"Ain't shit. I'm just getting my whip cleaned," Jermel answered.

"That's wassup," said Pig, joining in on the conversation. "What are you doing tonight?"

"I don't have no plans as of yet," answered Jermel.

"Where you been at? You didn't know that Scarface was going to be in town?" Pig asked. "He suppose to be performing with Backyard Band at the Black Scorpion. That shit is going to be off the hook. Every hood in D.C. is going to be there, and I know them broads going to be showing off with all kinds of skimpy shit on!" Pig went on enthusiastically.

"Yeah, actually I did know," Jermel answered. "What, are y'all trying to go or what?" he asked.

"What, am I going?!" said Young World all hyped. "Shit, I'm already there! Pig about to take me out to Pentagon City Mall now so I can get me something new to wear. I seen this black and blue Coogi sweatshirt in Macy's that I want to get. I'll probably just get some blue jeans and black Timbs and call it a day." "Jermel I know you're going to kill' em with your outfit," said Young World.

"You think I'm not," replied Jermel. "It's going to be a club full of top flight broads in there. I got to give 'em what they want." Jermel smiled as the thought ran through his head.

"I ain't going to buy shit," said Pig. "Fuck them bitches, I'm going just like this! Them hoes going to be trying to fuck regardless. Don't get caught up on them bitches and forget your surroundings. You know them bitches got kids and their jealous ass baby fathers are going to be there." Pig went on talking about the night, sounding angry at some of the haters that probably be there.

"Fuck them niggas," Young World said. "If they didn't want no one flirting with their bitches then they should keep their ass in the house."

"We going to be alright," said Jermel.

"The whole 7th St. is going," said Young World. "Black is suppose to drive his van over there. That joint hold like eight to ten people alone."

"Jermel I know you don't like letting anyone hold your firepower, but this is a special occasion," Pig said.

"I got you," replied Jermel.

"I'm trying to see what that H&K or that Mac 10 do," said Young World.

"Them motherfuckers almost bigger than you," said Jermel laughing. "Look, meet me in front of the playground at nine o'clock. I'm going to have something real nice for y'all," he told them.

"Alright," said Pig. "We about to hit that mall."

"Don't be late," Jermel told him. "I don't wanna be out here with all them hammers on me. Police been starting to fuck with me lately."

"Trust me," Pig answered. "I'll be there."

As Pig and Young World left to go on their shopping spree, Jermel was putting the finishing touches on his car. The sun baked the Armor All on the tires as he sat in the passenger side listening to the music of his choice. Spice One, 'The Trigger Got No heart' blasted through the speakers.

He understood that events like these warranted trouble at its fullest. He knew he had to stay conscious and on top of the night as it unfolded. Soon after his car was shining and ready to go, he decided to go home and chill before he got ready for the night.

As he drove, he thought about what he would wear tonight. Jermel was very fashion oriented and had an array of top designers in his closet to choose from. After many rambling thoughts, he remembered that he had a fresh Fila sweat suit that he had bought at Georgetown a couple of weeks ago. He mumbled to himself that he would wear that along with the classic butter Filas.

The day flew by as he tried to adhere to the schedule he had set out in his mind. He glanced at his watch to see that it was almost 7:30 in the evening. He knew that if he didn't start getting ready then he wasn't going to be able to meet Pig and Young World at the playground as he had instructed.

He jumped in the shower and got dressed before heading out the door to enjoy what the night had to offer.

Jermel arrived at the Rec to see Pig and Young World sitting on the hood of Pig's car smoking weed. They both had cups of Remy V.S.O.P. in their hands. Pig had the Hot Boys cd playing in his car just loud enough to be heard within a three foot radius. The streets were dark due to the young up-and-coming kids shooting out the streetlights.

This was a good place for them to meet because everybody hung out at the top of 7th St, and they were at the bottom. At the top it was like a block party. Everybody was in the street drinking, smoking weed, and dancing to the music they played from their cars. There were about twenty people up there, male and female, giving a pre-show gathering in the middle of the street. Jermel pulled up and parked his car across the street from Pig.

"What's up?" Jermel asked them. "How long have y'all been out here?"

"We been here for about an hour," Pig said. "We went got some smoke and Remy, then came over here to get our lungs right."

"Where y'all get the smoke from?" Jermel asked.

"We went up Hobart St. You know they got that skunk up there," Young World told him. "I'm about to roll this shit up now."

"Yeah we got to smoke that shit before we leave. We can't drive all the way across town smoking weed with guns in the car," Jermel told them.

"I dig that," Pig agreed. "We definitely ain't doing that."

"Let me see what you got for me," Young World said anxiously.

"Y'all go over and get them from under the passenger seat of my car," Jermel said.

Young World jogged over to Jermel's car and reached under the seat to find twin Mac 10's with extended clips. A grin spread across his face and a boost of confidence entered his heart when he laid eyes on the protection he was working with tonight.

Young World was Pig's little cousin. At thirteen he had already made his mark in the streets. He was with 7th St. with all his heart and had been recently labeled 'street certified'.

Young World put the two guns under his coat and walked back to where Jermel and Pig were.

"Pig look at this joint," Young World said, exposing the weapon with extra ammunition and handing it to Pig.

"This right here is what you call a lifesaver," Pig said, smiling as he took the gun. "Jermel you got to turn me on to your connect."

"If you're really into guns like you say you are, you'd be putting the work in to get them," Jermel told him. "Look, all you got to do is go out to Virginia and you can get all you want."

"How the fuck am I going to do that?" Pig asked.

"Grab a pipe head out there that has a driver's license and a clean record. Go to one of them pawn shops out there, pick out what you want, then send the pipe head in to buy it. They'll do anything for a couple of rocks. Once you get back to the city tell him to report it stolen," Jermel explained to him.

"Damn, I didn't know it was that easy," Pig said in amazement.

"A lot of things come to you if you use your mind," said Jermel. "You're supposed to know and have this shit. How are you going to be out here in the streets trying to bang with them little ass pistols and your enemy got shit with fifty shot drums on it," Jermel went on to say.

"Yeah you right. I'm out here bullshitting," Pig told him.

"The good thing is you still got plenty of time to get it right," Jermel reassured him.

"Maaaan, pass that jay over here Young World!" Pig exclaimed to his cousin.

Pig took a deep hit off the joint and tried to hold it in but started coughing. "This is some good shit," he said through more coughs.

"Fuck yeah! This shit got me feeling right," said Jermel feeling a bit high. "I heard some rumors that Lil Ty was the one that killed Man. Y'all keep your ears open to hear anything about that."

"You know we are," said Pig.

"Let's get finished with this shit and hook up with everyone else," Jermel told them.

They finished the last of their smoke and drank the remains of their cups before piling into Pig's car and heading to the top of the street where the rest of the guys from their street were at. It was a little after eleven o'clock and all the 7th St. gangsta's were getting prepared to leave for the show. The O G Grady had a short speech with them before they got in their cars to leave, telling them to make sure everybody stayed together and to watch each other's back. Soon they were loaded up and following each other to Sherman Avenue, in route to the outing.

CHAPTER 9

Big John listened to Frankie Beverly sing 'Joy and Pain' as the street lights reflected off his driver side window. The first red light he got to, he pulled out a small straw from his pocket along with a bag of dope he copped from one of his peers earlier in the day. He dipped the straw in the bag and took two sniffs of the dope before the light turned green. He drove off in deep thought wondering about what he was going to get into that night. He had been kind of laying low from the streets since the murder of the Jamaicans. He knew that there were more of them and they were most likely seeking revenge.

Big John sniffed as he felt the addictive opiate drain down his sinuses, relaxing his body. He decided to stop past Romaine's house since he hadn't seen her since the day she put her only son to rest. He wanted to make sure she was doing alright.

When he arrived he could see the televisions brightness through the living room window which assured him that she was home. He parked his black Cadillac Deville, went up to the front door, and rang the bell. Romaine looked out her large living room window to get a full view of who was at her door. She saw that it was Big John and swiftly made her way to the door and opened it for him. It wasn't odd for him to stop by to make sure that she was alright and to ask if she needed anything.

"Hey girl! What's up?" Big John asked her.

"Ain't nothing up. I'm just sitting here watching my show," she answered as he locked the door behind him.

Romaine led the way down the hall to her living room. Old re-runs of The Cosby Show was playing on the TV, and an open container of Chinese food sat on the small glass table that was positioned in front of the white leather sofa. It looked as if she was enjoying her down time. She was wearing a pair of black spandex, a long Georgetown Hoya t-shirt, and socks with fluffy pink slippers. Big John made a brief phone call while Romaine got back in her comfort zone, wrapping herself in the blanket that was on the sofa. She grabbed the remote and started flipping through the channels as Big John finished his phone call.

"So what you been up to?" he asked as he hung up the phone.

"I haven't been doing too much other than working and trying to keep up the strength to keep going," she told him. "It would be a little better if I had someone here with me."

"You got to get out of here sometimes," he told her. "I know I can't imagine what you're feeling because I never lost a son, but you're going to have to move on sooner or later."

"I know, and I try . . . but it's so hard," she said despairingly. "Ever since I was sixteen it's just always been Man and I. It's hard but I've actually been doing a little better here recent."

"What you need in your life is me," Big John said to her confidently. "You need a man."

"Please. You would be nothing but a problem for me," she said. "All of these dudes out here are the same. All they can do for a woman is give them a wet ass! I work too hard to let a man come into my life and bring me down," she told him seriously. "I date every now and then, but that's it for me."

"I guess you got a stereotype for all men?" Big John asked her. "As long as you got that block up you ain't never going to find a man."

"Don't get that shit twisted. I ain't even looking to get one," Romaine responded.

"As phat as you are I'm quite sure you won't have any problems when you do look," he told her.

"See, that's what I'm talking about," she responded. "All y'all men see is a phat ass."

Big John's pager went vibrated giving him the signal that someone wanted to talk to him. After looking at the screen to see who it was, Big John picked up the phone and called the number back. Romaine got back to watching TV as he talked on the phone. Big John got up and walked to the door leading to the back yard and smoked a Newport as he continued talking on the phone. He finished his call by saying, "I'll be over there in the next hour. See you when I get there." Smoke blew in the cold air as he exhaled it from his lungs. He flicked the cigarette over the fence into the alley as he turned to go back inside.

He hung the cordless phone back on the charger before telling Romaine he was about to go and he'll check up on her later.

She stood up and proceeded to walk past him to let him out. As she walked by Big John looked down at her butt and squeezed it. This frustrated Romaine all the more causing her to fiercely react by slapping him as hard as she could.

The slap set Big John off. He grabbed her and threw her to the floor, jumped on top of her, and held her arms down and she squealed and squirmed to get free. With the drug coursing through his system he got very aggressive and punched her in the face while tugging at her t-shirt trying to rip it off.

Romaine burst out in tears as she tried to fight him off. She could not believe he was doing this and anticipated the moment he would come to his senses and get up to let her go.

He tried to kiss her on the lips while holding her down on the floor. He could feel his erection coming on fast. The more she twisted and turned, the more aroused he became. Her shirt finally ripped displaying her red lace Victoria's Secret bra holding her luscious breasts.

"Stop! Stop! Stop! Stop!" she screamed and sobbed as he continued to attack her.

Big John was breathing hard and in a state of complete rage. He ripped the bra off displaying her breasts, which aroused him even more. He then reached down and in one quick motion grabbed her spandex tights with both hands and tore them down her thighs.

Romaine was losing it as she tried digging her fingernails into his face and neck. He slapped her with an open hand until finally she had to cover her face to shield herself from his violent blows.

He grabbed her spandex with both hands and ripped them the rest of the way off as she lay on the floor defeated. He tore her legs apart and spit on her vagina to get it wet and entered her, pumping hard over and over until he came and collapsed.

He stood up and looked down at her, coming to his senses, got dressed and walked out still in a daze.

She laid on the floor motionless, feeling defeated and completely violated with tears streaming down her face. Her sobs were silent but her heart was screaming and damaged.

CHAPTER 10

Cars stretched down both sides of the streets from the blocks to the club. The young boys and girls loitered in the parking lot, smoking weed while they waited in the long line to get inside. The night was cold and tension grew in the air as all the streets of D.C. gathered at the same location.

Everyone was dressed to impress. The guys wore the latest urban and athletic gear, and the ladies did their best to reveal as much of their body as possible without it being illegal. They had one goal and that was getting as much attention as they could. The whole 7th St. crew parked their cars next to one another. They were all feeling good from the weed and drinks, and were ready to go party.

They didn't waste any time as they locked up their cars to go inside. Jermel, Pig, and Young World lingered toward the back of the crew. They positioned their guns under the fenders of their car just in case they needed to get to them fast. Quickly they caught up with the rest of their homies and headed straight to the front door. Big Tim worked as bouncer for the front door. He was an older dude who had grown up on 7th St. and knew most of the youngsters' families. He usually always worked the door whenever any bands played.

7th St. always got in without waiting in line. They would get a cursory pat down, unlike the thorough body search everybody else was subject to. They all came in with small weapons such as knives and mace.

After they got inside, they all gathered to the far left side of the huge room where the band was set up and ready to play. It was packed from wall to wall with different neighborhood crews from all over the city.

Jermel scoped the place to see what familiar faces were there. As he looked around he saw Lil Ty with all his homies from 13th and Shepherd and glowered at them. There were about twenty of them lined on the wall in the back of the club. Jermel also saw members of different hoods like 640, 3500, 57th J-Mob, Barry Farms, and 5th N.O. . . . .

The crowd drifted to the front as the band members took their places on the stage. Bodies started moving to the beat as the band started playing.

"Jermel look behind you," said Young World.

"What is she doing here?" Jermel wondered out loud.

Jasmine had also come with her friends.

"Shit, I don't know but I'm trying to see what's up with that broad standing next to her with them tight ass jeans," said young World.

"Well let's go over and holla at them," Pig said to them both.

"Yeah. Alright, c'mon," said Jermel as he turned to walk in the girls direction.

"Hey baby!" said Jasmine when she saw Jermel. "You look cute tonight."

"Thanks," he said. "I didn't know you were coming here tonight."

"My girl friends talked me into coming. They always say I'm a home body and never go out with them, so I decided to come," said Jasmine.

"She's alright. Stop trippin," said Pig.

"Ain't nobody trippin. I'm just surprised to see her here," Jermel replied.

"Well she's here now, and they alright because they with us," Young World said. "What's your girl's name here?" he asked Jasmine, looking at the girl in the tight jeans.

"Her name is Toya, but why didn't you ask her?" Jasmine answered.

"Yeah, my name is Toya. Come ask me," Toya said, taking Young World's arm.

"C'mon y'all, let's go take some pictures before a crowd get over there," Jermel suggested.

They went into the picture room and got in line to take the pictures. The photographer had a setup with two backgrounds to choose from. One was with the sun setting behind D.C.'s Monument with the words 'Night Life' written across the top, and the other was a picture of a black BMW 850.

The DJ had the sounds of Tupac's 'Me against the World' playing for the enjoyment of patrons as they waited to take their pictures. Jermel watched as the group in front of them took their pictures. It was a group of ten, and some made signs with their hands as a representation of what street they were from.

When the group of ten finished, Jermel, Jasmine, Toya, Young World, Pig, and Jasmine's sister Alvina took two group pictures. After the group pictures, Jermel and Jasmine took a couple of pictures together. Even though he didn't like the idea of her being in an environment like that, he enjoyed her company more and more as the night went on.

They got the pictures and went back to the section where the band was performing. They got back in time to see what they had been looking forward to all night. The band had started playing tunes to Scarface's "My Mind Is Playing Tricks on Me". As the lights came up, Scarface walked onto the stage dressed in all black from head to toe. The crowd welcomed him by singing along with him as he rapped the lyrics to the song.

Jermel, Jasmine, and their friends were standing in the back of the audience, but Young World wanted to go up to the front where the rest of their crew were.

"Come on! Let's go up to the front!" Young World shouted.

"Jermel I'm not going up there in that crowd," Jasmine said as she turned to look at him. "You go ahead up there with your friends. We are going to be back on the wall."

"Alright. If you need me, you know where I'm at," Jermel told her.

"Ok baby. We are probably going to leave in a while anyway," she said as she grabbed him to pull him to her for a kiss.

Jermel, Pig, and Young World made their way back to where the rest of the 7th St. crew were. The sound of the music was like candy to their ears. Scarface's ruthless lyrics put the young street soldiers' souls in war mode more and more as he performed.

The crowd got rowdy as the challenge of what crew was the toughest presented itself. Pig looked over and noticed that Lil Ty and his crew had made their way to only a few feet from where they were at. The guys from Shepherd St. started getting out of control by dancing and purposely invading the space of those around them. Their energy shifted towards the 7th St. crew, nearly knocking one of them to the floor.

One thing led to another and in what seemed like an instant the two crews was in an all out brawl. Lil Ty swung at Jermel and caught him in the jaw causing him to stumble a little before catching his balance. Pig saw the whole scene unfolding and before Lil Ty could get another swing off, Pig was there throwing multiple blows in his direction.

Jermel recovered and followed Pig's lead, knocking Lil Ty to the floor and kicking him repeatedly as the bouncers came running through the crowd to break up the disturbance. The huge 300 pound man snatched Jermel and Pig, one in each arm, by the back of their shirts and carried them to the side door where he tossed them outside. Other bouncers were throwing everyone else out that had been fighting.

Jermel saw people running in the direction of their cars and knew what was up. Knowing that there was a mutual understanding between both sides, Jermel and Pig raced back to Pig's car to retrieve their weapons. Once the war started, it was all a matter of who could get who first.

As they ducked next to Pig's car they saw Lil Ty and two of his homies run through a row of cars that were parked, and watched closely to see which vehicle they got into. They continued watching as Lil Ty and his boys got into an old gray 1985 Mercury Grand Marquis with paper tags. The windows had black limo tint which prevented anyone from looking in. Young World had made his way to the car as well and soon they were all piled in Pig's car and in pursuit. Jermel kept his focus on the Grand Marquis.

The car sped out of the parking lot leaving a cloud of dust kicked up from the gravel. Cars were racing by as Pig waited for an opening in traffic so that he could catch up with the Mercury that Lil Ty was in.

The opening came and Pig sped out. They could see Lil Ty's car four cars ahead of them. They were able to see its tail lights through the trail of brake lights and watched as the right turn signal came on signaling that they were about to turn onto Florida Avenue from Bladensburg Road. One of the other four cars turned right as well as Pig turned behind them, giving a little space in traffic so they wouldn't be noticed.

"Pig pull up on them and let me air that joint out!" said Young World enthusiastically.

"Chill out shawty. We are going to get our man, you got to have patience," said Jermel calmly. "They are only about ten minutes from their hood."

"Yeah you right Jermel. They are going to feel like they safe once they get back into their area," agreed Pig.

Young World had the Mac-10 cocked in his lap as they cruised behind the Mercury, excited with the thought of using it.

The cool night air was hitting them in the face. They had the music off and the windows down so that they could pay attention to everything that was going on around them. Soon they were back on the Northwest side of town where they were from.

They watched as ahead of them the Grand Marquis pulled into the gas station on 11th and Sherman Avenue. Lil Ty and a tall light skinned guy, who could have easily been mistaken to be of Latin descent walked to the window where a plump woman sat behind a thick bulletproof glass.

Pig cruised by the gas station and parked at the end of the block. Knowing this was their chance; all three quickly got out the car and walked toward the gas station with their hands on their guns under their shirts. Pig jogged across the street to give him a different angle than Jermel and Young World.

As they were approaching Lil Ty spotted Jermel and Young World coming towards him and pulled out his Colt .45 Automatic from his waist. His partner that was with him pulled his 9mm Glock and the popping sounds began.

Pig sent a storm of bullets in the direction of the one who was pumping gas. He didn't have a chance as the hot bullets ripped through his body. The first shot hit his shoulder, turning him around as the second and third hit his chest. One of them pierced his heart. The life left his body almost instantly as he fell limp to the ground leaving the gas to continue pumping.

Both sides exchanged fire and did not let up but Lil Ty and his friend emptied their guns and was no match for the machine pistols their opponents brandished.

Lil Ty and his partner realized they were both out of ammunition at the same time they noticed that they had been hit and was bleeding badly, and tried to crawl for some type of cover. Pig and Young World ran towards them as fast as possible to finish them off.

Jermel stood back and watched as Pig emptied his gun into the Latin looking guy and Young World took Lil Ty himself. He stood back and surveyed the carnage in front of him and heard police siren approaching in the distance.

"Come on, we gotta get the fuck out of here! Now!" Jermel shouted to his friends.

They ran back to Pig's car, jumped in, and sped away. The entire incident only took seconds and adrenaline was spreading through their body like water as they drove off through the night, thoroughly satisfied with their work.

CHAPTER 11

The tension was thick as the days went on. There was always a constant gun battle going on between the two street rivals.

Early the next morning, Shepherd St. retaliated against 7th St. by catching one of their guys riding a bike. As the young man rode down the street a white Ford Bronco pulled in front of him and two masked men jumped out the back and shot the sixteen year old multiple times in the face and body. When they finished they jumped back into the truck and drove off, leaving the boy's young body lying in the street twisted under his bike.

The war was very intense, becoming a shoot-to-kill at sight situation. The fire was greatly fueled by Lil Ty and his partner Duke who got killed at the gas station.

Duke was related to the Speman's, one of the biggest families in Northwest D.C. There were a few of them living in every hood, and they were well known on the streets and in prison for the work they put in. The word on the street was that they were going to keep killing until all of 7th St was a ghost town.

Jermel, Pig, and Young World started spending a lot more time together. Jermel knew that he could no longer operate as a loner, and his friends had proved to him that they would put in work when it was needed. It left Jermel no choice but to trust them.

The beef went on to be on and popping, which meant more blood for blood. If Shepherd St. shed blood on 7th St., then 7th

St. did the same to Shepherd St. and this was happening more and more often.

Jermel stood at his front door waiting for Pig to come and scoop him up to take him to the car lot on Jefferson Davis Highway in Alexandria, Virginia. He had made a deal with the dealer to trade his Maxima for a 1990 Acura Legend. He had to trade in his car along with $8,000 for the deal to be final, so Jermel was taking him a payment of $4,000 to reduce his bill in half.

He had been shot at while driving home from Jasmine's house and he knew his car was hot so he had to get rid of it so that people wouldn't know what he was in.

Jermel looked out his front door and saw Pig pull up to the curb in front of his house. He noticed that Young World was with Pig as he locked the house door and ran down to the car to meet them. As he got in, Jermel gave them both a pound and they pulled off, on their way to the car lot.

As they started driving, Pig said, "Jermel I had that broad Rita from up Clifton Street last night in my mother's basement."

"You talking about Rita with the hazel eyes?" Jermel asked.

"Yeah I burnt that joint up last night," Pig said. "She told me to be careful when I'm with you because her cousin Chuck hangs on Shepherd St. with them dudes and she overheard her cousin and the dude Boogie talking about you. They were saying that you targeted Lil Ty because you found out he was one of the ones that came through and hit Man."

"I didn't even know for sure it was his bitch ass," Jermel said.

"They said they got to get you out of the way because they think you got too much influence," Pig told him.

"Fuck them bitch ass nigga's. They hit two of ours and we've hit three of theirs. The score is 3-2 our way," Jermel said smiling. "As soon as we get out of the city fire the trees up. I need something in my lungs."

It was only about a twenty minute ride to the car lot. Alexandra is on the south side of a bridge named after our twenty-eighth president, Woodrow Wilson. The bridge separates the nation's capital from Virginia.

Shortly after they crossed the bridge they were pulling into the car lot. Many of the young men from the D.C. streets would come to this car lot to get their cars. The guys than ran the car lot didn't care if you had good credit, bad credit, or even a drivers license. If you had the money, you were going to leave driving the car up to you. They would clean all the paperwork and make it look like you were completely legit and in compliance with all aspects of the law.

Pig parked near the entrance and they all got out to see what cars were on the lot before being approached by a short chubby Italian looking man who wore his hair greased back with gel. Jermel greeted him like he knew him and let him know that he was the person that he was there to see.

Pig and Young World was looking at a burgundy Range Rover and decided to climb into it and sit down for a closer look. Young World fantasized about owning the truck as Jermel and the man that looked like he was part of the mafia went into the dealer's headquarters. Pig and Young World jumped from car to car to explore their various luxuries.

When Jermel came back out they could see him smiling from ear to ear. He walked up to them and showed them the keys the dealer had just given him to the smoke gray Acura Legend that he was in the process of buying.

"Damn, how did u get it already? I thought you still had to pay four thousand," Pig asked.

"Shit, he liked my style," Jermel replied in a cocky tone. "I'm young and on top of my game, plus I made a deal with him that I would pay four hundred per week until I pay off the other four thousand. He is holding the title to the car until it's paid, and if I don't pay he gets to take the car back and keep my Maxima."

The wise dealer used this tactic all the time. In his eyes, the youngsters would either not pay the balance as agreed in the contract he had them sign, get locked up for some crime, or get themselves murdered. No matter what happened, the car would come back to him and the risk was well worth the benefit if that happened.

"So you get to take it today?" Young World asked.

"Yeah, he's going to let me take the joint. They in there right now making me some temporary tags," Jermel answered his friends.

"What are you going to do tonight?" Pig asked him.

"I'm going to swing past Jasmine's house and surprise her, then I'll probably take down to Georgetown to get something to eat," Jermel answered.

The dealer came out of the building with the temporary plate in one hand and a screw driver in the other. He put the tags on for Jermel in less than five minutes.

In a matter of moments, Jermel was in the car and off in a hurry with Pig and Young World following close behind. They got on Interstate 95 on their way back home and Pig pulled up next to Jermel and patted the accelerator as an invitation to race. Jermel hit his accelerator to the floor and shot off into traffic. Pig closed in on him within seconds as Jermel maneuvered through traffic in attempts of getting away from him. He was unsuccessful. The Legend was no match for the supercharged Grand Marquis, an old police squad car that Pig was driving. Pig tailgated him until Jermel put his left arm out the window as a sign of surrender.

Jermel took the 3rd St exit that took him to the intersection of New York Avenue. Jermel drove down New York Avenue feeling great. He'd have the car paid off in no time. To accommodate his good mood he turned up the radio as R. Kelly sang his favorite slow jam, "Honey Love" as he drove on to Jasmine's house.

Jermel pulled up to Jasmine's, he saw her, Toya, and Alvina on her front porch sitting in the swing chair that was attached. From the looks of things he guessed they were engaging in an activity that they referred to as 'girl talk'.

Jermel's presence interrupted their conversation as they stopped to stare, trying to figure out who it was that had just pulled up in a strange car.

Jermel got out of the car and walked up to the porch where the girls were.

"What's up Boo?" he said to Jasmine. "I don't get no hug?"

Jasmine stayed where she was sitting with an angry look on her face.

"Damn it's like that?" asked Jermel kind of surprised.

Jasmine looked up at him annoyed and answered, "I haven't talked to you in two days. Why don't you go back to doing whatever it was that you were doing when you couldn't call me back after I paged you." She stood up and looked at him. "You probably was with some girl in your little new car."

Jermel looked at her. "Man you trippin," he said. "I haven't been with no girl, shit has just been crazy these last couple of days."

Jasmine sat down and glared at him as she replied. "Whatever. I guess what was going on stopped you from calling me to see what I wanted. Anyway, you need to go check on

Romaine. She called me crying looking for you. That's why I been calling you like that."

"Did she say what was up?" Jermel asked, worried and wondering what was going on.

"She just said to tell you to come past there as soon as you can," Jasmine answered.

"Let me use your phone," Jermel said.

Jasmine went into her house getting a little calmer, and returned with the phone from the living room table. He immediately dialed Romaine's home phone which rang until the answering service picked up. He left a message for her to page him as soon as she got the message.

"Jasmine when she call you?" he asked.

"She called a couple days ago. I asked her was she alright and she said she just had a lot on her mind and that a lot is going on right now. She's probably worried about you because of all the drama going on around 7th Street," she told him, trying to relax after seeing how worried he became after hearing about the call.

"Naw, that don't sound like her. I got to catch up with her and see what's going on," Jermel said as he turned to leave. "I'll be back. I got to go check on her," he yelled over his shoulder as he jogged back to the car.

Jasmine watched him as he jumped in and drove off.

Jermel first attempted to find Romaine at her beauty shop. He parked down the street, but when he went into the shop she was nowhere in sight. He walked over to the older light skinned woman who was doing a little girls hair and asked her where Romaine was at. She told him that Romaine had left for the day, about ten minutes before he got there. He asked her to let her know that he came by if she happened to call or come back.

He left and drove towards Romaine's house. He felt a sense of relief when he spotted her tan Infinity Q45 parked in front of her house as he turned the corner onto her block. He quickly parked his car and ran to her door, knocking repeatedly for her to answer. She came and opened the door after she peeked through the window to see who it was.

"Romaine what's up?" Jermel asked anxiously. "Jasmine told me you was looking for me. That's my fault for not calling you to give you my new pager number. I lost my other one a few days ago."

"Don't worry about that," she replied. "But you need to come in here because I need to talk to you."

"What's up? Is there something wrong?" Jermel asked.

"This is about your fucked up ass Uncle John," Romaine answered. "Don't bring that motherfucker nowhere around or near my house again. If he comes over here again I'm going to blow his motherfucking brains out."

"I don't understand. What happened?" he asked.

Tears streamed down her pretty face as she looked away from him and tried to fix her mouth to get the words 'he took advantage of me' out. It was hard for her talk about it because it was like revisiting the horrible scene that she was faced with. It was hard for her to move on. She couldn't although she tried very hard to understand what she had done in her life to cause this chain of events to occur. First her son was torn away from her through violence, and now her womanhood was taken from her through violence.

She sat there silent with tears streaming down her face, still trying to comprehend why it happened.

Jermel put his arms around her with the goal of comforting her and asked again, "Romaine what's going on?"

She laid her head on his chest and sobbed as the words 'he raped me' came out her mouth.

Jermel held her tight as she cried on his shoulder and whispered to her that it was going to be alright.

For some reason Romaine felt better that Jermel was there. She felt like he was the only one that she had in her corner.

"Let me take you out to eat," he told her.

"That's probably a good idea because I haven't eaten in a few days," she said, wiping her face trying to relax.

"That's what's up," Jermel said. "And you'll get a chance to go for a ride in my new car."

They went to get Jasmine and rode over to Crisfield Seafood where they enjoyed the rest of the evening over lobster tails and crab legs.

Romaine began to feel better having a nice time with the people she loved like family. Jasmine even softened towards Jermel and they laughed and talked about good times.

CHAPTER 12

Police squad cars were at both corners blocking off the entrance to 7th Street. Two unmarked cars were in the middle of the street on the block.

Several uniforms and a few plain clothes policeman explored the area looking for guns or illegal narcotics. They had Grady, Wade, Donnie, and Young World face down on the ground while they searched.

Pac Man, an undercover officer given the name by the streets because of his speed and uncanny ability to chase you down if needed, came through the alley with Lil Freddie with his hands cuffed behind his back.

Lil Freddie had spotted the unmarked car coming around the corner and ran through the alley, disposing of his Ruger 9mm and a plastic bag filled with tiny pieces of crack. Pac Man saw him run and had unfailingly chased him down.

An undercover officer assisted Lil Freddie as he kneeled on the ground beside the others.

Officer Allen was one of the elder cops on the scene. He had been working the neighborhood for four years and was familiar with all the dudes that hustled on the block. He knew most of them by their street names along with their government to match. He had gotten the K-9 from the squad car and was walking him up and down the block. He knew there were drugs out there someplace, he just didn't know where. As he walked the dog beside the boys it stopped and pawed at the ground indicating that there were drugs nearby.

Officer Allen instructed two of the undercover officers to search the young males thoroughly to find the drugs. The officers searched each one individually by bringing them to their feet and leaning them over a squad car that was parked by the sidewalk. The officers made them put their hands on the hood and spread their legs. When they got to Young World and began searching him, he was dismayed to find that he could no longer conceal the rocks that had been squeezed between his buttocks because the officer had grabbed his pants by the waist and was now shaking them aggressively. He felt the small plastic bag that contained about ten small packaged rocks fall out of his pant leg and land on the ground in front of the officer. "Fuck," Young World thought to himself.

"We got us one!" said the short stocky undercover, as if had discovered a serial killer. He turned Young World over to one of the uniformed policeman to be placed in the paddy wagon, thoroughly pleased with himself for finding the rocks.

"Call my mother," Young World said as he was placed into the paddy wagon along with two pipe-heads that had been caught with drug paraphernalia in their possession.

When the police finished their scan of the area, they let the others go that they had temporarily detained. Pac Man said to them, "You all can go now, but I want y'all to know that we know what's going on around here." He started to walk off but turned around abruptly and said, "One more thing. Tell your buddy's Pig and Jermel that we got their sidekick."

The young men got off the ground, dusted themselves off, and walked down the street. Donnie went around the corner to Young World's house so that he let his mother know what had happened. He used her phone to page Jermel while she drilled him for details. Donnie waited for about twenty minutes for Jermel's call but he never answered the page. Jermel had been laying low. He spent his last few days with Romaine. Since she lived by herself he didn't feel right leaving her at the house alone. Jasmine would stop by every day after school to give her some company as well. She didn't know exactly what had happened but she could sense Romaine was having a hard time with whatever it was.

Jermel stopped going to school because of all the drama that was going on. He wasn't trying to make himself an easy target for his enemies by being where they expected him to be. He told himself that he wasn't going to get caught unaware of his surroundings like his best friend Man was on that fateful day in history.

When Romaine would go to work he would do a lot of thinking and wondered if he would make through the madness he was in. He often wondered how his life would be different if his mother hadn't passed away when he was just a baby. In way, he looked at that as a curse because he was subjected to his present way of life and blamed that on her death. On the other hand, he understood that making excuses would not help his present state and he had to be strong if he wanted to make it through the struggle. A struggle that got more and more intense with each day that went by.

He realized that he was too deep to turn back and his tenacity to overcome outweighed his enemies' persistence. His mind got stronger in a world that he felt like he was all alone in. Murder had become his best tool for overcoming the odds. Man was the only one that understood him but now that he was gone, anger took his place.

Romaine got better as the days passed by. Jermel being there by her side gave the boost she needed to keep going. Every time Jermel thought of what Big John had done it made him despise him more and more. To him Big John was no longer family. Jermel knew that he was ruthless and recalled the time when he was just eleven years old and was visiting John-John,

Big John's son, for the summer. Big John came into the room where he was watching videos on TV. and told him to come into his room. He recalled seeing coats and papers all over the bed as Big John said to him," Look you lil motherfucker, if I don't find my shit in the next five minutes I'm going to take you somewhere and ain't nobody gonna be able to find you. You think you're slick, but I know a lot of people in the street. I know you're out there trying to hustle and my shit ain't never come up missing until you came over here."

Jermel remembered pleading with him that he did not take the drugs but Big John didn't believe him and slapped him around then grabbed him by the neck and warned him not to play with him. Jermel became angry as the tears rolled down his face because knew that Big John was going to hurt him.

Jermel knew for a fact that Big John would indeed hurt him from all of the stories that he'd heard about him growing up, like the one about him cutting his brother's throat from ear to ear because he came in the house drunk and beat up their little sister Dee Dee.

Big John threw more things from the closet onto the bed in search of his drugs. He reached on top of the closet and pulled down a box that his wife kept her old purses in. He looked in the box and realized that the drugs were exactly where he had put them.

Jermel picked up the phone and called Pig to see what was going on. Pig filled him in on what happened to Young World and of all the gossip on the street. He told Pig that he needed him to meet him at the McDonalds across the street from Howard University in an hour. Jermel hung up the phone and got ready to leave the house for the day. He was dressed in all black, from head to toe, and tucked a 10mm Heckler & Koch Automatic into the small of his back. He didn't know what the night would bring.

As Jermel was leaving the house Big John was coming in to see his mother. He spoke to Jermel and observed his body language for any animosity. Jermel played it cool and acted as if he knew nothing. He didn't want to put him on guard.

CHAPTER 13

Young World, along with the two other men was taken to the Metropolitan Police Department's Fourth District. The paddy wagon pulled around to the back of the building and the driver drove up to the intercom speaker box that was on a five foot pole from the ground. The officer spoke to the dispatcher, letting him know that he wished to get in there with three detainees.

The huge brown garage-like door slowly rotated upwards allowing the officer to drive into its underground area. When it stopped there were two officers waiting inside of the unloading area to assist them with their prisoners.

"How many do you have?" asked the gray haired officer.

"It's just three back there," replied the man driving the paddy wagon.

"Oh yeah, I see one of them is a kid. Where did you get them from?" the officer asked.

"These three come from that 7th Street raid," the driver answered.

"I heard there's been a lot of killing in that neighborhood. These youngins these days don't care about life at all," said the old man, shaking his head.

The officers unloaded the older men along with Young World then gave them all a quick pat down before being taken inside. The officer took off the handcuffs and placed the two older guys in one of the holding cells. They took Young World and put him in a cell with another juvenile.

Young World looked around as he stepped into his cell and the strong smell of urine drifted into his nose. He noticed a young man around sixteen-years-old sitting on the bench that was welded to the floor. He was dark complexioned with six three week old cornrows going to the back. He gave Young World a nod as he took a seat beside him.

Young World had never been in before and all that went through his head was all the stories he use to hear on the block about how new dudes would get their shoes taken when coming through the bullpen. He was now face to face with the decision of how he was going to carry himself in there. Reality hit him as skepticism entered his mind. He knew that jail and the streets were two different playing fields. At 5 feet two inches and 120 pounds, he knew he was the underdog in an environment such as jail. He made up his mind that he wasn't going to compromise his morals and principles in any way and the he would deal with all opposition in a manly manner.

Hours had gone past and it was now 8:00 pm. Young World was now sitting on the hard steel bench in the cell alone. A female officer had come to get the other juvenile that he'd shared the cell with hours before. It started to get cold and he took his arms out of his sleeves in an attempt to keep warm. His back got stiff causing him to switch positions as a means of getting more comfortable, but to no avail. Every way he sat was terrible.

Young World grew impatient and began knocking on the door to try to get some answers as to when they were going to get him and tell him what was going on. He told himself that "this jail shit ain't for me."

Awhile later an older man that looked like he could easily be fifty came to the cell door with the same female officer that had come and taken his former cellmate out. They opened the door and instructed him to come to the door, turn around, and put his hands behind his back. While he was being handcuffed, the older white man who was dressed in gray suit pants and a white shirt introduced himself as Detective Carson from the Homicide Division. Young World wondered why a homicide detective wanted to see him.

They escorted him down the hall to a small room on the right side of the hallway. The room was empty except for a round brown table and three chairs. It resembled a room that could have been used for small conferences. Detective Carson told him to have a seat, that he'd be with him shortly, and walked off.

Young World was puzzled trying to figure out what the detective wanted with him since homicide detectives dealt with homicides and he knew that he was in there drugs. He was left in the room with his mind racing, trying to think what this man could possibly want with him.

Another hour passed before the detective came back accompanied by another detective who went by the name of Special Agent Green, Bureau of Alcohol, Tobacco, and Firearms (ATF) Federal Division. He was wearing a baseball cap with the letters A.T.F. across the front, black army looking pants, and a black t-shirt with the same white letters going across the front of it as his hat. They walked in, looked at, and closed the door.

Detective Carson sat at the table across from Young World and opened a file that he had brung in with him. "I know it's been a long day for you, so let's try to get this over with as quickly as possible," he said. "First of all, as I already told you earlier I'm Detective Carson from the Homicide Division and this is Special Agent Green from the A.T.F.," he went on, gesturing toward the other man that was obviously from the A.T.F. by all the labels on his clothing. "We both have a few questions to ask you and as soon as we finished you'll be processed and they will decide what they are going to do with you. Are you alright with that?"

"Yes sir," Young World replied.

"Did the officers already read you your rights?" he asked.

"Yes sir," Young World said again.

"Okay, then we are going to proceed," said Detective Carson as he pressed on a tape recorder. He pulled out some pictures of Pig, Jermel, Lil Ty, and Black. "Do you know any of these guys?"

"I know these three," Young World answered, pointing to Pig, Jermel, and Lil Ty.

"I take it you know that Tyrone, or Lil Ty as y'all call him, was murdered."

"Yeah, I think I heard about that," Young World stated.

"No, James Allen or Young World whichever you want to be called, you know he's dead because you are the one that killed him. Everyone knows 7th Street and Shepherd Street been beefin," the Detective said to him as if he was Sherlock Holmes.

"Man, I don't know who killed him but it wasn't me. Word on the street is he got killed late last night," Young World told him feeling a little worried inside.

"Let's cut the bullshit, I got two bullet shells with your fingerprints on them. This is your time to start answering my questions truthfully or spend the rest of your life in jail for first degree murder," Sherlock told him.

Young World just sat there not knowing what else to say to the men. The only thing he knew was that he didn't want to spend the rest of his life in jail.

"So who was with you when you shot Lil Ty?" he asked.

"I don't know what you're talking about." Young World replied, showing the fortitude of a soldier. Something told him the Detective was bluffing.

"Well you can play hardball if you want; my investigation is far from over. I already have a witness that tells me 7ᵗʰ Street and Shepherd St. got into a big fight at the club that you were involved in. I also have your fingerprints on the bullet shell I recovered from the crime scene. I also know that there was more than one shooter that night. All I need is someone to put you on the scene and that is your life," the detective said to him frankly.

"I'm not going to take up a lot of your time," said Agent Green. "I just want to tell you that we also know that your friend Jermel has possession of arsenal and illegal weapons. I can see you're not going to cooperate so I'm not going far into it, but keep in mind that I'm on your trail and that under federal law a gun is ten to life."

The two men looked at him trying to stare him down as if to show they were disgusted with him, but to him it looked more like they were constipated. They then walked out, leaving him to be taken to the processing room.

Five minutes later the same female officer took him to get fingerprinted. After being fingerprinted he was told that he was going down to Oak Hill Juvenile Detention Center until his court date.

Young World didn't care about going there. He had a big brother that had already been in there for almost two years for robbery and kidnapping. In his mind, the time would give him a few days to spend with his brother who he missed and tried to imitate in the streets.

CHAPTER 14

The temperature was dropping fast as the winter days came in. The chill caused Jermel to zip up his North Face ski jacket and put on his hood while walking to his car. He pressed the button on his key chain which unlocked the doors.

With all that was going on he had become very paranoid, making sure to look up and down the street to observe everything in sight before he got in the car. He wanted to give himself a fighting chance if an ambush came his way.

When he felt that everything was okay and that the coast was clear he got in his car and drove off slowly. The tint on his windows allowed him to hide his identity from the public. Even with it being early in the day Georgia Avenue was still live with heavy drug traffic on both sides of the streets as he cruised by.

After driving for a few minutes, he turned into the McDonald's parking lot to meet Pig. He saw Pig sitting on his car talking to two females. One was about 5 feet 6 inches, 130 pounds. She had caramel complexioned skin with shoulder length hair that was pulled back in a ponytail. The other one reminded Jermel of Nia Long, which caught his interest. They looked like two preppy college students that stopped to get something to eat between classes.

Jermel pulled his car in the empty space beside Pig's and put his window down, letting the sounds of MC Eight escape out of the car. The ladies took notice as the window came down displaying his boyish looking face.

"Hey boy, what's up?" Jermel asked. "I came over here because it looked like you had your hands full with these two sexy ladies."

"Yeah I think I might need some help because these two are something else," Pig replied. "They are from New York. They go to Howard."

"Oh yeah?" he said. "Brains and beauty, it's hard to top that these days." Jermel got out and leaned on his car while talking to them. "Excuse me for not introducing myself, I am Jermel and you are?"

"My name is India, and this is Keisha," the Nia Long look-alike told him. Keisha smiled as Jermel shook their hands.

"You look a little young, how old are you?" asked India smiling.

"I stopped counting when I became a man," Jermel answered boldly.

Pig smirked as Jermel talked to the girls, knowing he was time enough for their cynical attitudes.

"So are y'all going to let me and my man show you around D.C.?" Jermel asked.

"You must going to let me drive. You don't even look like you're old enough to have a driver license," said India in her seductive New York accent.

"She got a lot of jokes," said Pig.

They all smiled and chatted before getting serious and exchanging numbers. The two girls said they had to get to class and went on their way. Pig locked his car and got in Jermel's.

"Have you talked to World's mother yet about what they going to do with him?" Jermel asked.

"She told me that they sent him to the Juvenile Receiving Home," Pig answered. "He will probably be there until he goes to court. Shorty is going to be alright though, he's a little soldier."

"Well I know he's going to be alright, but we still got to go see his mother to show our loyalty. That's the first thing a person notices when they are locked up is who is by their side," Jermel told him.

"I feel you," Pig answered. "I wasn't looking at it in that way but I can see what you're saying."

"I just look at things for what it is. If I was locked up and the same people that claimed they fuck with me didn't even bother to see if I was alright, I would feel like they were fake and only dealt with me for their own hidden agenda. There is nothing sincere about it," he said.

"Yeah slim, you right," Pig agreed. "We got to keep this thing tight. I feel like we got to build that trust between us that cannot be broken. You and World are the only two I know I can trust in these streets. I know y'all got my back and I got y'all. You know them Shepherd Street dudes been coming through on the regular.

"That ain't bout nothing," he said. "We just got to go through there on a regular. Fuck them, they are not my concern. It's already understood what it is with them. My concern is the police. We got to stay two steps ahead of them for every step we take. Have they still been coming through the hood everyday jumping out?"

"Hell yeah, the block is on fire. I can't even make no money out there. I've been sitting in pipe head Angie's house, letting her go, out and bring the sales to me," he answered.

"Well that is the best way to hustle these days, you can't be on the block trying to get money and beefing at the same time. That shit really ain't going to work," Jermel said.

"Well what the hell are we going to do?" Pig asked.

"Let's get rid of all the coke we got left, take our money, put it together and go up to New York and get on. We can get a lot more for our money," Jermel answered.

"Man how the fuck we going to do that? We don't even know nobody up there," Pig told him.

"We don't need to know nobody. All we got to do is find our way to Spanish Harlem. Everybody out there is selling drugs," Jermel assured him. "That's the only way we going to get ahead. It's a chance that's worth it if everything works out."

"Fuck it. I'm in it if you are," Pig told him while smiling.

"Good. We got to get things in order so we can handle our business without being seen as much. Being seen out there all the time is just going to get us killed." Jermel said.

"I agree." Pig answered.

"All we will need is like five youngins and some good product then spot to push our shit. As long as we keep shit organized and stick to our plan things will work out much better. We'll stay safe and get more money." Jermel told him, laying out the plan.

Jermel and Pig were feeling good about their new plan. They understood they couldn't live their life day to day in the streets with no direction. They came to the realization that only two things would happen to them if they didn't change how they operated. Either they would get gunned down or end up doing years in prison on a charge.

The next few weeks they dedicated to getting their money together. They cut down on their spending, trying to make every dollar count. Jermel had talked to a few old heads to learn a little more about the New York City drug trade. He found out that they sold their product by the gram, unlike the way it was done in D.C. and for the most part the Dominicans up their were about money. They ran everything like a business.

Jermel liked what he was hearing and felt better and better about making the move as the days went on. He looked forward to the day he could go up there and bring back some good high quality product.

A couple of weeks before they planned to go to New York to get on Young World went to court for a bond hearing and the judge released him to the custody of his mother. He still had to go back to court to fight the case though since he had decided to take it to trial.

Since he decided to fight the case, he knew that he'd need a good lawyer. A good lawyer cost a lot of money that he didn't have, so he was excited about the plan that Pig and Jermel had cooked up. He was eager to get the money he needed.

CHAPTER 15

Pig came into Jermel's room with a black backpack hanging on one of his shoulders. This was the day they were meeting at the 'round table' to make the final preparations for their trip to New York.

Pig emptied the backpack onto the bed and a large pile of small bills tumbled out. It was mostly ones, fives, tens, and twenties, but there were also a couple of fifties and hundreds in the mix.

Jermel looked into his eyes then turned and went to the closet and retrieved a brown Timberland shoe box and carried it over to the bed. He opened the box and inside was stacks of bills neatly stacked on top of each other, sorted by denomination. They spent the next hour counting the money together, ending up with an estimated amount of $9,500.00.

"Jermel did you talk to your old timer Black about the prices up New York?" Pig asked.

"Yeah, I'm on top of all that. Black told me the average going rate is twenty one dollars per gram. We got a little over nine G's, how much are you trying to spend?"

"I don't know. What do you think we should do?" Pig told him.

"Well we can do two things," Jermel replied. "We can spend half, since it is our first time going up there and we aren't sure what we're getting into, or we can spend the whole nine so we won't have to go back up there."

"We might have to play it safe and spend like five of the nine." Pig replied. "You know anything might happen. We might go up there and get some bullshit. Even with spending just five we can still get like a quarter-key."

"You're right," Jermel said. "That's more than enough for us to get started with. I was thinking, and all we have to do is take four of the ounces and break them down in seven gram quarters. That'll be a quick four g's and most of our investment back. We can break the rest of it down into twenty dollar rocks," he said, doing the math.

"We got make our rocks big to cut out all the competition because even if we make fifteen hundred each off the other five ounces, we still will have like six thousand dollar profit," Pig told him.

"If we pull this shit off, we'll double our money and double it fast," Jermel said smiling broadly. "This plan sounds good. We can take that ten thousand and go right back up there and do it over again."

Jermel did you take that pipe head Angie to Romaine's shop to get her hair done like you was suppose to?" Pig asked him.

"Yeah, she is over at her house waiting on us. I also took her to the mall and got her something decent to wear," Jermel answered.

"That was a good idea to get her to drive us up there," Pig said. "She is old enough to be our grandmother, which will make our trip less suspicious on that hot ass New Jersey Turnpike."

They both planned to wear suits to make it look like they were going to a formal outing with a relative. Black had told Jermel of the stigma's that were put on young black males driving on the highway, especially Interstate 95 and the New

Jersey Turnpike that they had to travel on to get to their destination.

They put their street clothes in the backpack that Pig had his money in, and dressed in their suits. Before long they were off on their first mission to rise in the drug trade.

Angie was only about forty, but looked much older from all the drugs she had used over the years. She sat at her house waiting for the boys to arrive so she could take them on their trip. She was all for the trip because in her eyes she was going to come up all the way around the board. She got her hair done, a new outfit that she hadn't had in years, and a free trip. On top of all that, she knew they would take care of her when they got back.

Jermel pulled up in front of her house and blew the horn for her to come out. He got out the car and climbed in the backseat so she could drive. Angie came out of her house, locking the door behind her. Pig had to admit that Romaine had really did a number on her hair. He could see now why all the girls in the hood said that Romaine was the best in the city. Her hair was neatly styled back in a bob with the right side slightly longer than the left. She wore a tan pant suit that met the curves of her body. For the first time in as long as he could remember, she looked clean and sophisticated.

Angie got in the car and they were on their way. Jermel was anxious to get a good deal so that he could finally make some real money. He was tired of taking a lot of risks in life and not really benefitting. He now had a plan, and if everything went according to the plan he could get out of the streets by the time he graduated from high school.

After four hours on the highway, Pig and Jermel finally saw a sign that read 'East 125 Street Exit'. Jermel instructed Angie to take that exit. He had been told that 125th Street would take him right where he wanted to be. Angie had taken the exit and was now on 125th Street in Uptown Harlem. She turned on Lennox Avenue to get some gas at the station that was on the corner of 124th and Lennox Street.

Jermel and Pig got out and stretched their legs. Pig went to pay for the gas while Jermel stayed outside and pumped it. Jermel enjoyed the New York scenery as he looked into the bumper to bumper traffic. Everything seemed as if it was moving at a faster pace. It was after ten at night, but to Jermel it felt like rush hour.

Jermel had also noticed the drop in temperature. It had to be at least ten degrees colder than it had been in D.C. The first thing they wanted to do was get some of New York's best weed to smoke and find a place to stay for the night.

They all agreed to chill for the night and get a fresh start in the morning. Everything was going according to their plan and their next task was to get a hotel room for the night.

The street numbers went up as they drove north on Lennox Avenue. When they got to the red light on 143rd they saw a lit up red sign that read hotel hanging from one of the buildings on the street. They parked, grabbed their bags, and went into what looked like an apartment building.

A fat man sat on a stool at a window as they entered the front door. Angie did all of the talking and asked the man how much would it be for a room for one night. The man, who spoke to Angie in broken English, told her it would cost sixty dollars if they stayed until ten in the morning. Angie got the money from Jermel and paid for the room.

The man gave her the key, sending them on their way. The room was run down looking. It had two full sized beds, a dresser with a twenty inch TV, and a small round table with two chairs.

Pig walked to the window which had a plain view of the streets below. He could tell by all the noise and activity below that they were in the hood. It was mostly young people on the block. Some were black, but majority were Latin. They changed clothes and went outside to see what was going on.

"Let's go over to that pizza shop," Pig said, looking across the street.

"Alright let's go," replied Jermel. "We can ask one of them dudes standing beside the door where we can find some good weed."

As they approached the pizza shop, a young Dominican in his early twenties looked at them and spoke saying, "Yo what's good?"

The whole block was owned by his family. He already knew they were from out of town because of the car they came in. He even knew what hotel room they had rented. Even the pizza shop was a family business that was used as a front for their lucrative drug trade.

"What's up with you?" Jermel asked, stopping and giving the guy his full attention.

"I'm just out here on my grizzy," said the man.

"What's up with that chocolate," Jermel asked, speaking of what he had been told was the best weed in New York at the time.

"I got you bee," he said. "I got whatever you want. Where are you all from?"

"We from D.C.," Pig answered.

"Word," said the Spanish looking guy. "Just call me Tony."

"I'm Pig, and this is my man J," Pig told him gesturing at Jermel.

"How much of that are y'all trying to get?" Tony asked him.

"We just want a few nics to smoke," Pig replied.

"You know I got coke, heroin, and wet too," said Tony.

This was turning out to be easier than Jermel and Pig had imagined. They thought that they really had to find someone that could fill their order. They didn't know they could get anything from a five dollar rock to a kilo right on the same block.

Tony took them into the pizza shop and told the young female waitress in Spanish to give them whatever they wanted, on him. Jermel ordered a large cheese pizza with extra cheese. Tony told them to stay right there and he would be right back with their order of weed.

'Ay Pig, what do you think?" asked Jermel. "I think he's got that work."

"I do too," said Pig. "Let's see what he's talking about when he gets back."

Tony came back shortly and sat at the table while they were eating pizza.

"I told you I wouldn't take long homie," said Tony. "I put something special together for you since you're visiting."

Tony handed Jermel a small paper bag and told him to hurry up and put it away.

"So how much per gram of the fish scale?" asked Jermel. Black told him that was the best coke in New York.

"I got it for twenty-two a g," said Tony. "How much you trying to spend? I might can do something for you."

"I got like five g's," said Jermel. "Look out for me. I'm going o be fucking with you on a regular basis," he told him.

"You know what?" Tony asked. "I like your style. It takes balls to come all the way up here at your age. How old are y'all anyway?"

"Sixteen," Jermel answered.

"If I had the same drive at sixteen that you have, I'd be rich by now. I'm going to look out and do twenty a gram," Tony told him. "That's two fifty for that five."

Jermel and Pig had already done the math before they went to the city. Two fifty or better was what they were going to get for their money.

"That sounds good," said Jermel with a big smile on his face. "We were just going to chill tonight. How about we make this happen in the morning?"

"That's fine papi," said Tony. "Take my number and call me when you're ready."

Tony wrote down his number and left it on their table. He told them he would be waiting on their call. Jermel and Pig felt more confident as their plan unfolded. They understood the hardest part was yet to come, and that making it back with the drugs would be the riskiest part. They put the remaining pizza in a box for Angie, got her a drink, and went on their way.

Once they got back to their room, they rolled up the weed and smoked until they were too high to smoke anymore.

They went to sleep anticipating their big day.

CHAPTER 16

The trip to New York had been a success and was all in place for Jermel and Pig to start building their empire. Now, they just needed the people to work for them.

They had Young World get three of his peers that were trying to make money and were very hungry for it to join their team. Young World was in charge of the operation on the street, while Jermel and pig were taking care of manufacturing and supplying the inventory.

Tony admired the young boys' willingness to excel in this life of crime. It reminded him of when he was back home in the Dominican Republic as a young child. He couldn't wait for his chance to come to the States to make a life for himself, just as his father and uncles had done before him.

143rd and Amsterdam had been in his family since the early seventies. All the men in the family would get a three year run on the block. In order for anyone to stay after that, they had to start their own organization. That's exactly what Tony had plans to do. He saw potential in Jermel and Pig and had thoughts of guiding them up the chain which would in turn make him more money and expose him to another city in the States that he could move his work.

Tony gave them 90 percent pure cocaine that would surely make it hard for his competitors. He had seen fire in Jermel's eyes when he told him he could make him rich if he stayed consistent in buying from him. Tony had told him everything that he wanted to hear.

Jermel and Pig's goal was to find a good connect. They were aware that the only way they were going to get ahead was though a reliable supplier with good product. Jermel learned that a few years ago when he use to hear his man Black plan trips to California and New York to get his work. Black would always say, "if you really wanted some money then you had to take chances." Finding a good connect out of town was the hustler's dream from D.C. The city's drug market was mainly controlled by out of towners with an enormous amount of product. With a tight grip on the market and prices higher than other cities, it made it hard for the lower level slingers to get ahead. It didn't take long before survival of the fittest became the law of the city. Murder, robbery, and trickery became the only way to survive.

Jermel and Pig understood what they were up against. They both understood that if word got on the street that they had been going to New York to get on, they might be a target. Their plan was not to let that get out. The only people that knew were Pig, Young World, Angie, and Jermel. Pig told Angie that if their business got out or if anything unusual came their way; he was going to have to deal with her.

With the first package that they brought back from New York, Jermel and Pig spent hours breaking the cocaine down into little stones that would be sold for ten and twenty dollars apiece. Young World would meet them every morning and get one hundred dime rocks and twenty rocks that were individually packaged in tiny bags. They had put together a system for Young World. He was to place his three youngsters in the spots designated on the block with small pocket-size walkie talkies. One on each corner watching for the police or anything suspicious, and the other in Angie's house selling the product. Young World's job was to oversee everything and make sure it ran smooth.

Jermel told him to only put twenty rocks each in the house at a time. Angie's house was an already known crack house, so it didn't look odd for crack-heads to frequently visit her.

In just two short weeks, things were starting to really pick up. All the crack users in the area had started to hear about the quality of crack they were selling. The traffic slowly picked up as the days went on. The money was coming so fast that Jermel and Pig deviated from their original plan. They sold the entire crack in little ten and twenty dollar pieces, which gave them more of a profit than they had expected. After all the crack was sold, Jermel, Pig, and Young World set up a meeting at Pig's house. They had a saying that said 'going around the table'. That meant they would meet up to count their money and discuss whatever it was that was on their mind.

Their operation was running smooth, and so far everything was going according to plan except that they were making even more money than they had expected to make.

It was a rainy Wednesday with Jermel, Pig, and Young World absent from the classrooms they were supposed to be in. The three were instead smoking exotic weed and listening to the Ghetto Boys in Pig's mom's living room. The three took a seat at the kitchen table and started to count the money that they had made in the days before. Jermel told them to make thousand dollar piles. They counted sixteen thousand in all. Jermel and Pig stayed focused, knowing this was just a start while Young World saw the piles of money before him as a fortune.

"Jermel did you call Tony and tell him we were coming to see him?" Pig asked.

"I talked to him before I came over here. He said that he'll be ready for us when we get there," Jermel answered Pig.

"It ain't no need to keep bullshitting. Let's get something bigger this time," Pig said enthusiastically.

"You just read my mind," said Jermel, agreeing with him. "Let's take this sixteen up there and see what we can get for that. Angie said not to get it already cooked up no more. She said we could come out with a lot more if we did it ourselves, and she said she could do it for us."

"You think that bitch know what she's doing? Don't want to fuck it up," said Pig.

"What pipe head don't know how to cook coke," stated Jermel sarcastically. "All we got to do is let her cook a couple of grams first and then put them out as testers to see what her friends say."

"We can give it a try," said Pig. "It makes a little sense now that I think about it. Our goal is to make as much money as possible after all."

"Look at it like this," Jermel told him, "All the extras we get from cooking it go to our workers."

They had their workers that were under young World on a five hundred dollar a week salary. Everybody was eating and happy about their role in the conspiracy to come up.

While Jermel and Pig made plans to go see Tony, Young World made his way back out on the block to make sure everything was going according to plan.

CHAPTER 17

The cigarette burned between his fingers as the two inch ash dangled and fell into his lap. Big John sat in a rental car outside the Bank of America on Connecticut Avenue, nodding out from the dope he sniffed minutes before with no regards to life. He decided that it was time for him to get some money and to get it fast. The ten to forty thousand dollar capers from the streets were not cutting it anymore. He felt like he was getting too old to be out in the street and needed to make a quick come up.

He figured that if done correctly, he could take five banks for a hundred thousand apiece. His plan was to leave town afterwards, only to come back to visit his mother and kids. He had done so much dirt in the city that he knew his time was coming.

Sometimes he wondered about how he was still alive when he had been face to face with death on so many different occasions. Every night it got harder and harder to sleep, and his mind started to play tricks on him in a way that made him constantly anticipate death. Big John came out of the nod and observed the activity in and outside of the bank. He watched as the elderly man got out of his gray Chevy Impala. The man walked to the box beside the front door and pressed the numbers that turned off the security system. Big John had been casing the spot for a few days now and would soon make his move. For this kind of caper he knew he needed an experienced getaway driver. That was the only thing holding him up. He had a couple of people, but he wasn't sure who was really fit for this type of job.

He let his thoughts run their course through his mind for a few more minutes while he checked out the scenery up and down the block, taking a mental note of what was going on. He had made that his early morning homework for the past week and felt that this was going to be an easy one.

He put the car in drive and slowly blended into the morning rush hour's traffic. Big John told his man Beanie he was coming over to talk to him. They were both trying to figure out who was behind that bomb coke that was being sold on 7th street. Everybody was talking about it. They knew Jermel and his crews were selling it, but Big John wanted to know who was behind the scenes giving it to him. He had no clue that they were making everything happen themselves.

Beanie knew that Jermel was Big John's nephew, and he wanted to see if he could get Big John to talk to Jermel into setting up his connect and splitting the lick down the middle with him. Big John pulled in front of their new get away spot on the 500 Block of Long Fellow Street, Northwest. Big John quickly made his way to the front door and let himself in. He knew Beanie was inside by noticing that the car that he'd been driving was parked down the street as he drove by. He smelled a strong incense aroma mixed with weed as he walked down the hallway into the living room where Beanie was.

"Beanie, what's up partner?" asked Big John as he took a seat on the couch.

"I'm just sitting here thinking about what I'm going to get into," Beanie answered. "I might take this broad out to the mall. She be fucking with that credit card shit. My baby-mother been sweating me about buying my son some new clothes."

"Yeah, well what's up with that shit you was telling me about last night?" Big John asked.

"Man, I don't know where them youngins getting that coke from, but they got that shit on lock on 7ᵗʰ Street. That's all motherfucker's talking about," said Beanie.

"It's got to be somebody around the way," Big John said. "They don't know no one like that on that level."

"I think they know somebody because they been having that shit on the regular," said Beanie. "You got means of finding out. Shawty looks up to you. It would be an honor for him to put in some work with you. You better get on top of that shit," he told him.

"I don't know slim. I think shawty might be a little fucked up with me; you might have to shoot your shot. You know he fucks with you, so just tell him that you just came across some money and you're trying to invest."

"That might work," Beanie answered.

"Make it seem like you're going to give him the coke to sell to give him the incentive to fuck with you. He'll see that as another come up. He's always been into making another dollar," Big John said.

"I'm going to call him and tell him to meet me somewhere to talk," said Beanie.

"Yeah, and when you see him give him an ounce of that good green you've been in here smoking," Big John said smiling.

The plan was to find out who was the man behind the coke. Big John and Beanie knew that whoever it was, they had to be a heavyweight in the drug game. Dealers these days couldn't afford to sell their coke this pure unless they had a whole lot of it. Usually if someone came across some good coke, they would cut it to get good product. The quality was usually degraded as it came down the chain of command.

The youngsters had switched the game up to their advantage. If they kept getting that good coke, soon everybody would have to get with them to make some money. Not only was everything going according to plan for Jermel, but it was also looking good for Tony as well.

CHAPTER 18

Jermel felt the pager at his waist vibrate repeatedly against his belt. He was driving his car on his way to the corner store at 14th & Fairmont Street where he got the miniature bags to put the coke in. He looked down at his pager and saw that it was Jasmine paging him again. She had been getting upset for him not calling her back.

Jasmine could see a big change in Jermel. When she would page him he would take hours to call her back, if he called her back at all. She was insecure in their relationship because of it, and began to often accuse him of being with another girl or not spending any time with her. To her, he had made a huge change in his demeanor. He seemed not to care about her the way he use to and it was tearing her up inside. She would sit at home and wonder what she had done to him for the treatment that she was receiving. She felt alone and distant from the first and only boy she ever loved.

Jermel had no idea she felt the way she did. He felt he had love for her, and to him, that was all that mattered. Spending time with her was not his main priority; his love for making money was consuming all his thoughts. The streets had become his main focus and getting rich was his goal. He knew he had to stay on top of things and be innovative in the way he ran things to keep it all running smooth. The coke was moving so fast it kept him busy most of the time that he wasn't asleep. He didn't want Jasmine to feel neglected, but getting his money together was his top and only priority at this stage of life. His plan was to get in, and back out as fast as he could. He didn't want the label of being 'the man'. He knew that being in the spotlight only brings heat from both the law and the street, the two entities he always had to watch his back for.

So far, everything seemed to be running perfect. Things seemed to just fall into place when they needed them to. Jermel and Pig had just come back from their third successful trip to see Tony. Their relationship with him was getting stronger with each trip. Tony was really starting to feel that he could trust them. He also recognized their potential and was using it to his advantage by giving them whatever they needed from him on consignment.

This was a huge boost in business for him. Jermel and Pig started to sell weight to the other young hustlers that hung out on 7th Street, and now had two different crack houses that were bringing in sales of a few thousand each and every day. Jermel and Pig put up a front like they had met some Africans that had the coke they been selling. They told everyone that if they wanted the coke they had to buy from them because the Africans that were supplying didn't want to be seen or to meet anybody new.

The others in the street didn't really care where it came from. They were just happy to be able to get the product because everybody in the hood was making money off of it. Jermel tried not to let what was happening go to his head. He knew that what was happening would not last forever.

After paying all their workers and giving Young World $6,500 to pay for his lawyer to help him win his case, Pig and Jermel had about $35,000 between the two of them. They knew they had a long way to go.

Jermel began to talk to Pig about doing something legit with their money. Romaine didn't like the fact that Jermel was in the streets doing what he was doing, but she understood that most youth saw the streets as a way to get rich quick and were willing to suffer the consequences.

Jermel was too deep in the street for her to try to get him to turn away, so she used a different approach. She made him aware of the fact that most of the time people who seem like friends turned out to be enemies. She told him to have a plan that included the day when he had to leave the streets for good and decide how he would invest his money when he did.

Jermel took heed to everything she had told him. He knew that she had told him everything she did because it was in his best interest. He made a vow to himself to get out when he had made a hundred thousand for himself. He figured that would be enough for him to start the business venture of his choice when the time came. He was thinking hard about teaming up with Romaine to open another beauty salon.

Jermel's pager went off again, instantly changing his mood from what it was. He figured it was Jasmine paging him again to give him a hard time about not being with her. He frowned as he looked down to see the number on the screen. The strange number turned his expression from annoyed to puzzled. Not only did he not know who the number belonged to, but at the end of the page was a '911' indicating that it was an emergency. Jermel wanted to know what the 911 was about so he picked up his car-phone and dialed the number as he drove through traffic.

"Hello," answered Beanie.

"Yeah, did someone page me?" Jermel responded feeling a bit irritated.

"This Jermel?" Beanie asked.

"Yeah, what up," he replied.

"Jermel, hey this is Beanie. I been trying to catch up with you so I can holla at you about something. I saw you the other day and tried to stop you, but you didn't see me and kept going," Beanie said.

"Holla at me about what?" Jermel said, still irritated with the interruption but curious about what Beanie had for him.

"Look shawty, I came across a little something that you might want. Come past my spot, I'm at 735 Longfellow," Beanie told him.

"Give me like ten minutes. I'm right up the street from you," said Jermel, no longer really bothered but more excited. The first thing that came to his mind was that Beanie had got his hand on some new guns. Beanie only liked hand guns, so whenever he got anything else he would sell them to Jermel. This would be right on-time if he did have some. Jermel rushed over to see what Beanie had on his mind.

When he got to the house, he went inside and sat down to listen as Beanie gave him the spill about how he wanted to buy some coke. Jermel knew the story didn't sound right because he was not a hustler; he robbed people to make his living. Beanie told Jermel he had ten thousand he wanted to put in the coke and flip because he heard how good it was and knew it could be done fast.

"Man who you getting that shit from?" Beanie asked.

"I met these Africans downtown," said Jermel.

"When can we hook this up? I need to make some extra money to send my oldest daughter back to college. That shit is fucking expensive." Beanie stated.

"You got the money right now?" Jermel asked.

"Young Blood, I'm ready," Beanie told him.

"Alright, I'm going to talk to them and see what they can do for the money you got. I'll be back over here later on to let you know what's up," Jermel told him, knowing that Beanie was up to something shady.

"Alright, good looking out," Beanie said. "So you know, the money belongs to me and your uncle, I'm going to tell him I talked to you and everything is set in order."

"Alright that'll work. I'll see you later on today when I find out what's up," said Jermel.

Jermel left the house thinking to himself about how the timing could not be any better. He needed very much to take care of that business with Beanie and Big John, and they had just made it way easier than he thought it would be.

CHAPTER 19

When money is being made in D.C., dislike and hate comes from every direction. The growing envy was causing trouble in the hood. In the past couple of weeks there had been two robbery attempts and a drive by shooting, which resulted in an innocent bystander getting graced.

Young World made sure he put protection on their investments. He knew that as soon as people realized how much money was being made out of the houses, it was going to be a problem. No one on the street wanted to see the next man succeed in any way. They'd rather that both fail instead of just the jealous one.

Jermel knew that his worst opposition was going to come from the inside of the hood. Most of the people that got robbed on the street found out about the information from an inside source. He faced the reality of everything that came with his operation and he was prepared to deal with it. Being careful was a must for him, one slip up could cost him his life, and he knew it.

Jermel kept his ear to the street about the situation with the Shepherd Street guys. Word was that they were going to chill for a while to let the heat die down. The homicide detectives had been pressing them about the murder of Man, and they wanted things to cool down.

Their plan was to rock 7th Street to sleep, letting them drop their guard down so that they could have a successful offensive. The way it was now, they knew they would not make it.

Being aware of what was going on was a must for Jermel and Pig. They had talked and understood how important it was for them to get rid of their enemies so that everything in their operation would run smooth.

Jermel felt that he couldn't start off better than dealing with Beanie and Big John, giving them what they had coming. He knew that they would become a problem if he didn't give them what they wanted which was their supplier, and he had no intention of giving them Tony.

Pig and Young World were waiting patiently for Jermel at the Gorn's Café. He was supposed to meet them there, and they had been waiting for a while. They didn't mind waiting though since he had told them he needed to talk to them about something important.

He arrived a few minutes later and walked inside, spotted Pig and Young World and sat down with them at their table to talk.

"It's about time," Pig said. "We've been here for almost an hour."

"My bad," Jermel said. "I had to trade cars with Grady for today, and I had to take him all the way over Southeast to get his car."

"I'm just saying, you made it seem like it was an emergency or something like you needed us," Young World spoke up. "I got this .40 on me because I thought it was a work call."

"It's work call every time you come out your house," said Jermel grinning as he thought about how big Young World's heart was to be so young. He knew he wasn't that advanced at the same age.

"What's up?" Pig asked. "What's going on? You got some news from the street or something?"

"I think that dude Beanie who hangs out with Big John is trying to bring me a move," Jermel started. "He called me out the blue and told me to come and see him, so I went over there and he says he wants to buy some coke. I found it odd because I know he don't he don't ever fuck with that shit."

"That shit don't sound right," Pig replied.

"I'm hip; he kept asking me who I was fucking with. On top of that, he said the money was his and Big John's and I just seen Big John and he did't tell me anything like that all," Jermel said.

"I think Beanie's grimey ass is on some bullshit," Young Word cut in.

"Yeah he still on that 70's ass game, but I got a plan for his slick ass," said Jermel grinning. "We are going to beat that motherfucker at his own game."

"I'm with it," said Pig enthusiastically. "If we are going to have any success with all this shit, we can't have any picks. We got to deal with whatever situation that comes our way."

"That's right," said Jermel. "That's how you get power in the streets. We got to let it be known that its consequences with trying to get in our business, How you think the mob is so powerful? That's another thing I wanted to bring up with you Young World. Make sure you instill in them youngins you got on the block the importance of protecting the block and dealing with infractions harshly."

"I'm on top of that," Young world told him. "The last time some dudes came around there trying to do a drive by, my youngins chopped that car up so much it surprised me to see them all on the same page like that."

"Good, I like hearing that," said Jermel.

"Grady's lil brother, Bubbles is going to be a beast!" said Young World. "Shawty is trigger happy for real. All the others kinda look up to him. They're all out there trying to prove that they are on the same level as him."

"It's all good and fine to have heart, just make sure they are not out there being reckless and bringing heat on us. Make sure you stay on top of them," Pig told him.

"I told you, I got that under control," Young World assured them.

Jermel, Young World, and Pig decided to order something to eat since they were already there. They were regulars there, so the waitress knew what each of them wanted to eat without them having to tell her. They enjoyed their meals while discussing their plans for Beanie and Big John. Jermel knew they had to come up with something fast, because Beanie was waiting on his call. The whole thing had to be finished before the day was over.

When they had finished formulating their plan, Jermel instructed Pig and Young World to get ready. He instructed them to park their car in the hood and let them know that he would be there to pick them up in a half hour.

Jermel watched as they left the parking lot, walked to the payphone, and dialed Beanie's number.

"Yeah?" Beanie answered.

"It's Jermel, what's up?" Jermel talked cool with the plan running through his mind. "I talked to my people. I need to meet with you. They want me to see the money then call them after I make sure everything good, and they'll come over and we can do business."

"Alright I'll be here and have the money here," Beanie said thinking he had gotten over for sure.

"Alright I'll be there in like an hour."

"Alright, I'll see you then," Beanie said, hardly containing his excitement.

"Oh, have Big John there since it's his money, too," Jermel reminded him.

Jermel felt good at the fact that Beanie seemed completely oblivious to what was really going on. He quickly left the carry out to pick up Pig and Young World, feeling like a true mastermind as he drove.

When he arrived on Taylor Street they were there waiting for him. Jermel pulled up to the curb where they were standing, and unlocked the door so they could get in.

Jermel updated them on the phone call, and the rest of the ride was silent except when Jermel stopped to go in his house saying he had to go get something special for the job. He came back to the car without any apparent change and calmly started driving again.

When they got to the street where Beanie's house was, they looked around the neighborhood and found a parking space a few houses down from Beanie's. It was a quiet street with well kept row-houses lining both sides of the street.

As they sat in the car, they discussed the plan one last time before they carried it out. Jermel said, "Okay, it doesn't look like Big John is here yet, I don't see his car. I'm going in, remember when you get a page with all seven's on it that is your sign to come knock on the door."

"I got you," said Young World.

"Pig, give him five minutes before you come to the door," instructed Jermel.

He got out and made his way to the door and rang the door bell. Beanie looked out of the peep hole anxiously and let him in.

"What's up shawty," Beanie said. "You are a life saver. I'm glad you came through for me. Your uncle ain't here yet, but he on his way with the money." He took another hit off the blunt he was smoking before passing it to Jermel.

"That's what family is for," Jermel said.

As they walked to the living room Jermel scanned the house to make sure he was truly alone. "This shit got me high as fuck already," Jermel said, playing it cool.

"I got plenty of this shit," Beanie told him. "Don't worry, I got you. One hand washes the other, you know."

When he was sure the place was empty, he said," My man said he's going to do something nice for that money. I told him you all family and you were cool, but he still told me to be with you and check things out before we do the first transaction. That way y'all can meet and exchange numbers too. How's that sound?"

"Shit, I respect that. He sounds like a real business man," Beanie said.

"Well let's get this shit over with. He told me to page him so I could tell him where to meet us. Where is your phone at?" Jermel asked.

"On the kitchen table," Beanie said, smoking the blunt again.

Jermel went in the kitchen and grabbed the phone and dialed Young World's pager, then pressed seven, seven times to notify him to do his part. He then put the phone down and waited.

Young World's pager vibrated as he sat in the car waiting. He looked down and saw '7777777', and knew what to do. He walked to the door and rang the door bell.

Beanie opened the door expecting it to be Big John but was instead met by Young World asking to use the bathroom.

"I got the shits man, let me use your bathroom. I can't hold it man," Young World said, faking sickness.

Beanie laughed and pointed the way to the bathroom. He didn't know Young World, but had seen him with Jermel numerous times and knew he was cool.

Young World passed Jermel on his way to the bathroom and nodded. Jermel said to Beanie, "Call Big John and tell him to hurry up so everything is in place. My man is going to call any minute and will be here quick and will want to handle business as soon as he get here."

"Yeah alright, pass me the phone so I can get on top of that." Beanie took the phone from Jermel and called Big John feeling like it was his last barrier between him and a sweet come up. His plan was to do a small deal with Jermel's connect today to gain his trust, then they would rob him next week on a much bigger deal and have a huge come up.

He hung up the phone and turned around smiling to tell them Big John was on the way, but was met by the blue steel of Young World's .40 caliber in his face. "Get on the floor bitch!" Young World shouted.

Beanie was stunned and high. He didn't know what to do, so he got down on the floor as commanded. He didn't see this coming.

Once he was on the floor, Jermel opened the front door and Pig walked through the door with a backpack on looking like he was coming home from school. They opened the bag and retrieved the gray duct tape and wrapped it around Beanie's head, covering his mouth. They then taped his hands to his feet behind his back, securing it so he could not move or get free.

Beanie's eyes were wide with fear as he heard Pig ask where Big John was at. He heard Jermel tell him not to worry, he was on his way. He tried to struggle against the tape and quickly realized it was a fruitless endeavor and was quickly met by a boot to his face for his efforts, knocking him out cold.

With that part of the job done, Jermel picked up the blunt they had been smoking and lit it up to wait for the man who was once his role model, that he was now filled with hatred for.

"C'mon, let's put this bag in the basement," said Pig. "Jermel, stay up here and wait for Big John to get here."

"Okay, do y'all need help?" Jermel asked.

"Naw, we got this motherfucker," Young World replied as he started to drag Beanie to the basement door. Pig opened the door and Jermel watched as Young World pushed Beanie through the door and heard him bounce down the stairs, smiling at the sound.

Jermel waited in the front room until he heard the door bell ring. He answered the door calmly and saw Big John on the other side holding a bag, which he assumed had the $10,000 in.

"What's up?" Big John asked walking in.

"Not shit, just waiting on you. My man is on the way. We're all waiting in the basement for you. Beanie's down there with some killer green. Why don't you go down there and wait with him? When my man gets here I'll tell him everything's good and bring him to you. You got the money with you right, because he's bringing that work," Jermel said.

"Yeah, in the bag here. Thanks for setting this up shawty," Big John told him, thinking his plan was working perfectly. He would soon be surprised Jermel thought to himself.

Jermel watched as Big John walked to the basement door and walked down the stairs. As soon as he was out of view Jermel pulled out his silenced H & K USP 9mm Tacticle Pistol that he had picked up from his house. He had paid dearly for the gun and was glad he was going to use it on Big John.

"What the fuck!" he heard Big John shout from the basement and heard him run up the stairs. He was ready and fired twice hitting his uncle in the leg, taking him down as soon as he came around the corner.

Young World and Pig quickly grabbed him by the feet and dragged him into the basement, letting his head bounce off the stairs as they took him down. Jermel followed with his gun at his side.

"No, no, no!!! Please! Please!!!" Big John begged, in agony from the gunshot wound in his leg.

"Fuck you, this is for Romaine you fuck." Jermel put the end of the gun to his forehead and pulled the trigger twice, ending his once hero's life. He did the same to Beanie who still breathing slowly, and said "Pig grab the bag, it's got the money in it. Retrace your steps and wipe down anything you touched. Let's get out of here. We got to be seen someplace public."

They left the house and drove back to their block happy with the way things had turned out, and $10,000 richer.

CHAPTER 20

Jasmine stared at the walls of the small classroom as she sat at her usual set at the front of the classroom beside her closes friend Toya. Miss Wilson, an elderly woman with a stern demeanor, taught the class the property of triangles in her trigonometry class. Jasmine normally gave the teacher her undivided attention but today she was in a world of her own; Jermel was stressing her out with all the drama she's been hearing about in the street. Another worry was the fact she is two weeks late from having her period.

A tear rolled down her cheek at the thought of her becoming a statistic just like so many of her peers. She wanted better out of life and worked hard for a better outcome. Even though she didn't know for sure if she was actually pregnant, a part of her told her she was from the two consecutive days of morning sickness. Today she had planned to cure the curiosity with a home pregnancy test.

"Jasmine what is wrong," said Toya concerned.

"Nothing I was just thinking," said Jasmine.

"Girl, lets go to the bathroom cause something is wrong, you are not sitting in here with tears streaming down your face for nothing, it's Jermel isn't it. You need to stop messing with him, you can do much better."

The two young girls walked out of the class room and rout to the girls' bathroom. When they got into the huge hallway that lead to the restroom Jasmine broke down and cried, her hands covering her face. Toya stopped and wrapped her arms around her to comfort her.

"What's going on," said Toya

I think I'm pregnant she sobbed," I'm like two weeks late from having my period and on top of that I've been throwing up the last couple of mornings.

"Damn Jasmine, girl you messing up, you don't need any kids right now, you still have another year in school to go that doesn't even include four years of college."

"You act like I planned this shit!" Jasmine snapped.

"I'm not saying that you did," stated Toya as she rubbed her hair so that it laid neatly on her head. Since we been little girls all we talked about was how we were going to be successful business women. Remember all the conversation that we had about the strong black women of our time like Oprah. We can let the adversities of life get us off track."

"Have you told Jermel yet?" Toya asked

"I didn't want to mention it till I knew for sure," Jasmine responded.

"When are you gonna get tested? There is no need to keep procrastinating, you need to know so that you can weigh your options." Said Toya

"Your right, will you go with me today after school?" said Jasmine

"Of course I will, meet me at the front entrance after seventh period," said Toya.

After school, the two girls stood at the intersection on Kansas Ave on their way to the CVS to get a self pregnancy test. As they crossed the street Jasmine notice two young males in a black 300zx waiting for the light to change, the driver, a light-skinned guy with a curly afro stared at her as if he knew her. She didn't think too much of it because boys always tried to talk to her on a regular basis. She turned her head as if she didn't see him; Jasmine wasn't in the mood to be bothered they soon crossed the street and made their way on Webster St in silence. They made it half way up the block when the same 300zx raced up behind them, pulled up to the curve and jump out of the car.

"Aint your name Jasmine?" said the curly hair guy.

"Why?" said Jasmine in a smart way.

"Yeah! you that bitch that fuck with that punk ass nigga Jermel," the guy said. "I should put these hollow points in you since your scare ass boyfriend is hiding out."

"You ain't gonna do shit to her," said Toya.

"Bitch shut up cause you can get it too, I'll leave both ya'll asses here stinking, you don't know who you fucking with," he said. "Look, tell you little love that Zach from Sheppard St. said he's a dead man."

The two dudes got back in the car and sped off in a hurry.

"Girl you crazy," said Toya. "Jermel ain't all that to be going through all this shit. Ain't no way I would put myself out there like that. What if he would of tried some thing for real?"

"I know what you are saying but it's too late for all of that now," said Jasmine, "I love him and I'm gonna stay with him no matter what. True, he's not living right but I know he has potential. I also know that he loves me."

They continue to the store aggravated by what just happened. When they arrived at the store Jasmine scanned the shelves for a home pregnancy test until she found the one of her choice. She wanted to make sure that she bought the one with the highest accuracy rate.

The closer Jasmine got to her house more and more anxiety came upon her, she wanted to just take the test and get it over with. The girls opened the door to Jasmine house and headed straight for her room. Jasmine didn't waste any time and hurried to her bathroom in her bed room. Toya took a seat on her bed and waited for her return.

"What is taking you so long?" Toya yelled.

"I'm waiting for the thing to tell me if it's positive or not," said Jasmine.

"Girl let me in," said Toya, "why you got yourself locked in there?"

She let her in as they both watched the plus sign on the small plastic meter turn red giving the indication that she was pregnant. Toya could already see the tears welding up in her eyes as Jasmine looked at the reading on the test.

Jasmine's mind blanked out as reality set in, she knew that crying wasn't gonna help the matter go away. With all that was going on in her life she knew there were some serious decisions that had to be made.

CHAPTER 21

The next few days Jermel felt unsure of whether his ethics were completely moral or not. One part of him wondered if what he had done to his family was really the right thing to do. He knew that he was the cause of the Johnston family feeing bad because their loss. He had been home when Mrs. Johnston received the news about her son, and watched as she dropped the phone and started to shake. He thought she might have been having a nervous breakdown, and it pained him to watch her feel the power of the karma from all the evil that Big John had done.

On the flip side, Jermel felt that she would be able to now live a stress free life not having to worry about the well-being of her son. Big John had shattered his own blood from the way he had been living.

The bottom line was that Jermel felt sorry for Mrs. Johnston and her loss, but Big John got exactly what he had coming for the life he lead. He weighed the good his uncle had done, which wasn't much, against the bad and remembered how Romaine had broke down when she told him about being raped. He went on remembering how Big John had accused him of stealing his drugs and choked him for no reason. Basically in his eyes no man who abuses children and takes advantages of women deserves to live. Bad things happen to bad people and overall he was glad he had been the one to make it happen.

Young World was starting to understand the power that he held. He felt like the streets were his and no one could get in his way. Everything had seemed to fall into place. He hadn't seen all the work and planning Pig and Jermel had done to make it all happen, all he saw was that money was coming from everywhere on 7th Street.

Pig and Jermel were having to work harder and harder to keep Young World grounded. It was a must to them that he stick to their plan. Their vision was for them to jump in and out without ever being noticed. They had plans for bigger and better things. The drug money was just a way to get something to invest in something more profitable.

It was a Friday afternoon with traffic as busy as usual on the block. Young World had just passed out the last packs of coke that he had with him at the time. Everything had been running smooth and he knew that he had to re-up on his product. Friday's were now doing over four thousand a piece in each one of his crack houses. That wasn't including the orders he filled from the dudes on the corner, which was another couple thousand.

There was a lot going on and it was becoming too much for him to handle, only he didn't see it that way. In his young mind, he was unable to comprehend the vision that Jermel and Pig had in mind. All he wanted to do was stay fly and spend time with his girlfriend Shanita who was older than he was and would run circles around him. He would take a lot of his share of the money they made and blow it on her. She was high maintenance, and at sixteen she was already a gold digger.

Young World was intimidated by her and felt like the only way to keep her was by buying her nice things and dumping money on her. He had just turned thirteen and never before had a real girlfriend, so he didn't see what was really happening.

To him, she was the greatest thing that had ever happened to him.

Jermel and Pig began to notice how Young World would go missing for hours, bring in short money, and was not keeping the houses stocked up like he was suppose to. They had a talk to decide what they were going to do, because all they had built would go down the drain if Young World kept acting like he had been.

"Hey Pig, I know Young World is your peoples and all, but he's been fucking up bad," Jermel said.

"Yeah I know. That lil motherfucker had me go all the way over Southeast to get him from his girl's fathers house, and when I get there he tell me he can't go because she didn't want him to leave," Pig replied.

"He got his first piece of in house pussy and he don't know how to act," said Jermel. "I went around 7th Street today to talk to Angie and she told me that fiends been knocking on her door all day looking but World didn't put no work in there. She said she paged him but he never called back."

"You know what we got to do," said Pig. "We got to cut him off and let him get a taste of what it feels like to be broke again."

"I love him to death, but he needs to wake up and get focused on the plan," said Jermel. "I already talked to him three times about this shit and it ain't getting through to him."

"Fuck it, let's put Lil Duke in charge of the houses," said Pig. "Shawty be out there everyday faithfully. I think he can keep shit on track. Remember this is our chance. We got everything working in our favor right now and I'm not going to let Young World or nobody else fuck this up for us."

"You right Pig, we got to do what's in the best interest for us. World's my little man and I want him with us, but I can't let him take us down," Jermel agreed.

They did just what they had discussed. Lil Duke stayed on top of his duties. Things got back on track and the money kept growing. From the outside looking in, Lil Duke was able to understand where Young World had went wrong and he felt good to be in position to make more money than he had been while doing less work. He didn't have to stand on the block no more dodging the jumpouts and late night stickup boys. His chances of getting killed or locked up just went down dramatically. Jermel was all for putting Lil Duke in charge. He had seen something in him. Beside him having heart and not going for anything, he would always listen and do what he was told. The money didn't go to his head either. You would rarely see him in new clothes and splurging his money. He watched his brother mess his money up for too long and vowed that would never be him.

Young World felt some kind of way about them not letting him take part in the operation. In a way he felt like they had betrayed him. To him, the work he had put in should have overridden any amount of money that he owed. His whole young life he had been taught to always be true and loyal to his family and friends, but he felt like it wasn't paying off.

Young World took the little bit of money he had left and decided to try to flip it in some weed. He started selling weed to all the guys on 7th Street, and while he wasn't making as much as he had been selling crack it was enough for him to stay afloat and take care of what meant the most to him . . . his girlfriend Shanita.

CHAPTER 22

It was about four o'clock on a cool Friday afternoon. The kids filled the neighborhood after a long, tiresome week at school. This particular Friday on 7th Street, like all others, was alive. Bells rang as the small ice cream truck made its way around the block and the small children ran to get in line to be served. Ironically, at the same time, the area was manifested by pipe-heads running to the small level drug dealers like they were the ice cream truck to get served as well.

Young World was standing on the corner talking to two high school females who had stopped by to see him on their way home to get some weed. He had started to become known for having weed in the neighborhood, and more and more people in the hood started to get their weed from him. It was convenient for them because they didn't have to drive all the way up Hobart St. just to get high. Young World started to feel good about his operation and even started to think it was a good thing that he wasn't fucking with Jermel and Pig anymore.

He didn't make as much now as he did when he was working with them, but he felt like he was now his own man and he could do what he wanted to do. The only responsibility he had was himself. No longer did he have to get up early in the morning so that he could be on the block to pass the work out. He now got money on his own terms, and the best thing of all to him was that he could now spend as much time and money as he wanted with Shanita who at this point in his life meant more than anything.

Young World saw an ambulance stop at the red light across the street from him with its signal on indicating it was about to turn onto 7th Street but didn't think anything of it. He kept talking to the girls in front of him, and in the blink of an eye the ambulance came to a screeching halt about 50 feet away with men jumping out the back wearing all back ninja-like uniforms. Before Young World knew what was going on he was on the cement looking up at the letters DEA written across the front of some guy's shirt. Police squad cars and undercovers assisted as they quickly swarmed the whole block. Heavy guns were drawn as they took control of 7th Street like a hijacker on a 747 commercial airliner.

As they searched Young World, they found the .40 he had in the small of his back along with ten small packages of weed he had in his pocket. He was then placed in handcuffs and taken to the nearest squad car.

Young World sat in the back of the car as the reality set in that he was once again about to get locked up. The DEA was conducting a sweep that resulted from a twenty-two name indictment handed down from a grand jury that had been convened on 7th Street's behalf. They were filling up the squad cars and the paddy wagons fast.

They ended up detaining eighteen people that ranged in age from thirteen to forty, discovering over ten firearms and a few ounces of crack. They were all taken to the 4th District Police Station and placed in holding cells.

Young World sat on the concrete slab in the holding cell disgusted with life because he got himself caught up. As he sat there all he could think about was how Shanita was going to feel about him being locked up. He knew that this was not going to be good for him. He had only served six months of his two year probation that he'd been on for the first drug charge. On top him violating his probation, he just got caught red handed with a gun and more drugs. He collected his thoughts as he contemplated what his fate would bring.

As he sat there he heard an older black woman shout "James Allen!" and realized that she was the police officer working behind the desk at the present.

"Yeah I'm right her," said Young World as he walked up to the bars so she could see him.

"Let's go. Somebody wants to see you," she said, opening up the cell so he could come out. She took him to a small room with only a small table and three chairs, and locked him inside of it. As he waited he wondered who wanted to see him, two men he recognized walked in.

"Mr. Allen," said Detective Carson with a smug look on his face. "I see we meet again."

Detective Carson and Special Agent Green closed the door behind them and had a set across from Young World. "This time the ball is in our court," said Mr. Green. "Before we ask you any questions we are going to give you a few minutes to think."

Young World just looked at the floor with his head down not knowing what he should do. He got the vibe that they know what they know.

"Look son," said Detective Larson. "We know you're not an angel but we're not out to get you. We know you're young and just got caught up with the wrong crowd. Help us so that we can help you."

"How can I do that?" asked Young World.

"Who was with you when you killed Lil Ty?" asked Detective Larson.

"I didn't kill nobody," said Young World.

"Look you little dumb motherfucker, the lady that worked in the fucking gas station said you shot him right in front of her! In plain fucking view! When a jury hears that, your ass is going down! Don't fucking play with me. I don't have time for your games," said Detective Larson. "As a matter of fact come on Agent Green, let's go and let this little smart ass rot in jail," said the angry detective.

"No wait," said Young World as be began to cry. "It was me, Pig, and Jermel."

The two cops smiled as the young boy made his confession. They already knew who it was, but the lady was only able to identify Young World. That was all they needed to seal their case. The feds had already come back with an indictment on drug conspiracy charges. That, along with the murder charges of Lil Ty, the officers hoped to put the 7th Street crew away for a long time. Pig had also been picked up at his house by the drug task force a little while after they did the sweep on 7th Street. They went to Jermel's house but he wasn't there. As soon as they found him their work would be done, but what they didn't know was Angie had already warned him and told him to get out of town. Jermel took her advice and decided to leave town. His plans was to lay low until he found out what was going on. He made a call to his man Duck from Virginia and told him he was coming down there to hang out with him for a few days.

Jermel played it safe in Virginia with his buddy Duck. Duck didn't know what was going on with him back in DC, he use to run guns up there a couple of years back. He and Jermel had formed a good relationship. Jermel would buy a big portion of the guns and became one of his best customers.

Jermel called around to get as many answers as possible. He needed to know more details about what was going on. He talked to Pig's mother Goldie, and gave her the number to reach him. She said she would call him as soon as she talks to Pig or got more info about the situation.

"I need some fucking weed," Jermel thought. With all that was going on, he just wanted to smoke a fat blunt and contemplate his next move.

CHAPTER 23

"All rise and remain standing as the Honorable Judge Spencer enters the courtroom," said the court bailiff.

Goldie felt butterflies in her stomach as she stood to her feet. She knew a lot of the activity that he was involved in. Shame came upon her as she thought of how she could have been harder on him about staying out of the streets and going to school, but instead she let the fact that he was dropping hundreds off when she wanted it sway her parental authority.

"United States versus Tyrell Frye," said the young Euro-American woman.

Pig was escorted into the courtroom by two federal court Marshalls, arm and arm. He took a quick stare into the body of the courtroom for any familiar faces. A feeling of guilt entered his mind when he caught eye contact with his elderly mother. Pig knew that if he got convicted of any of the charges that he was facing, he probably wouldn't make it home before she passes away.

He took a seat at the long cherry oak table beside the young female public defender that was assigned by the court to represent him in his arrangement.

"Mr. Frye, please stand for the Court," said Judge Spencer. "Are you on any medications or drugs at this time Mr. Frye?"

"No your Honor," replied Pig.

"Very well," said Judge Spencer. "We are ready to proceed with the hearing. Mr. Frye, you have been charged with Count 1-841, Distribution of Cocaine Base; Count 2, 922g Possession of a Firearms By A Convicted Felon; Count 3, 924g Use Of A Firearm in Furtherance Of A Drug Trafficking Crime."

"How do you plead?"

"Not guilty Your Honor," said Pig.

"The Court accepts your plea, Mr. Frye."

"Is there any bail recommendation from the government?" asked Judge Spencer.

"Yes," said the prosecutor.

The short fat man stood up from the table to the right of where Pig was sitting. He shot him a stern look before he gave his request to the court.

"With all due respect to the Court, I think it would be an injustice to the taxpayers of our community to allow Mr. Frye the opportunity to be released prior to his trial. Mr. Frye is a known street thug that runs with the notorious 7th Street crew who has terrified the Petworth neighborhood. He has been named as one of the ringleaders along with another close associate who hasn't been apprehended yet. Mr. Frye is also named as the shooter of the murder victim in Court #3."

"Okay, the Court will take that into consideration. Is there anything from the Defense?" the Judge asked.

"Yes, if I could use a moment of the Court's time," said the Public Defender. "Your Honor, my client has always lived in the District with no history of missing court dates. Let's not forget that he hasn't been tried for any of these crimes and should be presumed innocent until proven guilty. I ask this Honorable Court to set a bond for my client in this matter."

"The Court denied bond and sets a preliminary hearing in this case for January 15th. The defendant will be remanded in custody until then. Next case . . . ."

Pig whispered to his mother who sat a couple of rows behind him that everything was going to be alright as he got up to go back to the holding area.

"Call me," said Goldie.

Pig nodded his head to give his mother the o.k. as he walked through the back of the courtroom.

As Pig sat in the dirty holding cell that was often called a bullpen, all he could think of was how things were happening so fast. He knew the feds had to have some real evidence to get involved. Somewhere down the line, they got statements that were helping them. He wanted desperately to talk to Jermel to hear what was going on and being said in the street. The streets will surely be talking once the word spreads of what happened on 7th Street. That was one thing Pig knew to be true. With Jermel still on the streets, he felt confident that he would hold him down as much as he was able.

Pig eventually broke out of his deep daze and shouted, "Bitch hurry up and come get me out this dirty motherfucker!" as the tall masculine woman officer walked past the bullpen

The two officers argued back and forth about which football team was better between the Redskins and Dallas on their way to Oakhill Juvenile Center. They were given the assignment by their superior to transport Pig to the Facility. Pig sat in the back of the police cruiser with shackles on his legs and his hands cuffed to the front of his waist. Pig was tired from the long day at the court building. He had been there since 6:00am which quickly turned into 8:00pm. Sitting on the hard concrete slabs for hours with no way to get comfortable really got to the detainees who had court dates. The smell of piss and shit didn't help the situation either.

He watched traffic from the window as thoughts of his fate entered his mind. He wondered about how much evidence the Feds had on him. One thing he knew he had in his favor was they didn't find anything on him or at his house at the time of his arrest, which was a good thing. That factor along with knowing he only put work in with his man Jermel and Young

World gave him confidence that he was going to be alright. Trust and Loyalty are the principals they stress which gave him a sense of relaxation.

The Officer made a left turn shortly after he passed a big green sign on the side of the narrow street that read District Of Columbia Department of Corrections Oakhill Juvenile Center 1 mile. They soon pulled up to the facility which was surrounded by a ten foot fence with razor wire loops covering the top. Pig was exhausted from such a long day. He wanted nothing more than a bed to sleep in. With all that was going on he hadn't had any rest for the past couple of days, anticipation of the outcome of his court date would not allow him to. He wished to have learned more at the hearing about what was really going on. Instead he was only read his charges and told he was going to have to stay in custody until his next court dates which was a couple of months later. He knew this was just part of the game and he had to remain strong.

Pig stayed in unit 10A for two days until he was told he would be going to unit 7B. Pig couldn't wait to get there because he really wanted to see his cousins Chase and Young World.

Chase was Young World's older brother. He was serving Juvenile life for a robbery and murder, committed when he was only fifteen. Young World was only ten years old when he got arrested but heard many stories about his street reputation and wanted to be just like him. Pig and Chase were the same age. They were more so like best friends than anything. Pig would often think back to the day when Chase robbed old timer Jay-Jay. He knew in his heart if he would have been with Chase that night he could have stopped him from killing Jay-Jay. The rumor was, Jay-Jay had already given him the money but Chase was trigger happy and still put two bullets in his head.

Chase has been down Oakhill for like two years now. He earned respect there as well. He only stood 5'6 130pounds, but his fight game was above average, which made his stand out from a lot of the other imamates that were there.

Pig walked through the door in unit 7B and went to the counselor's office to get his room number as instructed. A fat light skinned man named Simms told him he was in room 17 which was on the other side of the dayroom. As Pig walked towards his room he was tapped on the shoulder by Lil Freddie.

"Pig What Up?" said Lil Freddie

"Whats Up?" shawty I didn't know you were still here," said Pig embracing his hand.

"Yeah, I've been down here since that day they found that work on me in the hood. "What's up with you?, I heard they came through the hood and made a sweep."

"Yeah, they got me from my house," said Pig

"The hood is on fire right now. It's all stemming from all that gunplay we've been having with Sheppard St."

"That shit has even spread down here," said Lil Freddie. It's like six of them down her. Now that you are here, our numbers have gone up to five."

"What unit is World and Chase in?" Pig asked.

"World is on the other side in 7A and Chase is in 8B. Come on lets go see if we can find them. I think they are on the basketball court," said Lil Freddie.

Lil Freddie led the way as they went on a hunt for Young World and Chase. Pig wanted to see Chase but he really wanted to know what happened to Young World when he went to court. He was hoping he could learn more than he was told at his court date.

The rec area was filled with the young boys. Some were playing basketball while others watched the highlights of the game. Groups of them were scattered off in different locations of the yard as will.

Lil Freddie scanned the yard to see if he saw any of his homies on the yard. If they were not on the court they would always sit on the steps that led to the school building. It was no sign of them nowhere on the yard so they decided to wait until they went to the cafeteria when dinner was served.

Pig went back inside and got situated into his room while he waited to see Young World and Chase. He knew by now they heard he was down there. They probably couldn't get to him yet, was his guess.

Pig walked in the line in route to the cafeteria with his unit. When he made it to the entrance he noticed that it was a long line before him waiting to get their trays. The young boys were loud and rowdy. Before Pig could get his tray, there had already been a fight which was quickly defused by the staff that was on duty.

Chase and Yong World sat at a table close to the front. They knew Pig was coming and prolonged their meal so they could have time to talk to him.

"There he is coming in," said Chase.

"Pig !" yelled Young World.

"What's Up?" said Pig smiling. "I'll be over there in a minute. Save me that seat beside you."

"I got you," Chase said.

Young World checked out Pigs body language, he knew what he told the feds was against the rules and wished he could take it back. He felt bad he let the feds win him over in the interrogation room. The pressure was a little too much for him. Pig didn't show any signs that he knew anything which made him feel relieved.

Pig got his tray and walked to the table where they were. Chase stood up and gave Pig a hug showing that he really missed him. Pig felt good to actually see him in person. It's been two years since they seen each other but they have talked on the phone many times. Pig would always make sure he gave Young World money to take home to his mother for him.

"Man what's up?" said Chase. "What are ya'll out there doing to them Sheppard St. dudes? They hate everything that comes from 7th St."

"We been getting at them dudes," said Pig, "It's like an on sight shoot now ask later wild west type thing."

"I see, I had to knock a couple of them out down here," said Chase laughingly.

"They feel some kind of way about their man Lil Tye getting killed. A lot of them looked up to him," said Pig. "He had the most heart out of all them."

"World, what's up with you?" said Pig. "What did they say when you went to court?"

"My lawyer didn't show up so they postponed my court date for two weeks," Young World replied.

"I got to talk to Jermel, I know he has heard what's going on in the streets," said Pig. "When I talk to my mother I'm going to make sure she gets in touch with him. I can't stop thinking about this shit."

"You can't worry about something you don't have any control of," said Chase," Just chill out everything going to soon come to light."

Young World felt like his words was directed to him. His young conscience was eating him alive.

Chase filled Pig in on the do's and don'ts of Oakhill. Though it was a juvenile facility, it was notorious in its own way. The young boys there were in an unstoppable power struggle. Toughness was respected above everything. It was inevitable to be tested. In order to be respected they must prove they were not going to accept being violated in any way. Among many, the most common tests was someone attempting to take their shoes or at shower time not allowing them to get under the water, shower time is when the most fights would happen. Ten boys would shower together with only five shower heads so they would have to rotate and share the shower. If they detected weakness, getting under the water would not happen.

CHAPTER 24

Ring . . . . Ring . . . Ring . . . "Hello," answered Jasmine.

"What's up boo, how are you?" Jermel asked.

"Don't call here with that Boo shit! Why haven't you been returning my phone calls? You got everybody calling here telling me all this shit about the feds is looking for you. I've been worrying myself to death wondering if you were alright," Jasmine said, as tears began to roll down her cheeks.

"Look man I know shit has been fucked up lately, but a lot has been going on. I'm out having to watch my back; Pig and Young World are locked up. The feds did a sweep around 7th St., and on top of that it's a rumor going around that I killed this dude from Shepherd St. so I got to watch my back from that too," said Jermel.

"You still could have returned my phone call," she shouted back through the phone.

"You think it's all fucking about you! I guess you'll be satisfied when I'm sitting somewhere talking to you on the phone and somebody sneak up and put a fucking bullet in my head! Or better yet, the feds run down on me and I'm sitting in a jail cell," he shouted.

"All I wanted to tell you was that I'm pregnant," she said sobbing.

Jermel paused, feeling bad for not calling her back. He couldn't believe she was pregnant with his child. He wanted a child to love and provide everything that he wanted for himself. He loved Jasmine with all his heart and felt bad for the way that he had been treating her.

"Hello . . . Hello?" said Jasmine.

"I'm here. I just can't believe you just said that you're pregnant. How long have you known this?" asked Jermel.

"It was about a week ago, but that don't matter. What am I going to do? You know I'm trying to go to college next year," she said.

"We are going to be alright. I can't really tell you what to do, but I can assure you that I'm going to be the best father I can be for my child."

"Jermel how are you going to raise a child roaming the streets like you do? At the rate you're going you're going to be in jail or dead before the baby is even born. I'm against killing my child, but at this point I don't know what I'm going to do."

"I respect that," said Jermel, "but like I said, I'm going to be the best father I can. I can't promise you what's in store for me. Right now it's a lot going on in my life. I chose a lifestyle at a young age that has followed me for life, its called survival. I refuse to let the streets get the best of me. You got to understand that it's too late in the game for me to decide I don't want to play anymore," he said.

"Why can't we just leave?" she asked. "I'll have the baby and we can move away. I just don't want nothing to happen to you," Jasmine continued sniffling between words.

"Look, just give me a little time," said Jermel. "I'm going to make this better for us."

CHAPTER 25

Jermel had been out of town for a couple of weeks now. He thought that by now it should be safe enough for him to back to the city to see what the word was on the streets. Being away from all the drama gave him a chance to think about how he would move from that point on. After reflecting long and hard about everything, one thing would not change and that was he was not trying to go to jail at a young age having the system raise him into a man.

Jermel took Tony up on his offer to come up to New York for awhile until things cool off. Tony had called wanting to know why he hadn't heard from him. Jermel filled him in on a little of what transpired over the past few weeks. Unknowing to Jermel, Tony wanted him up there to keep him close to him and to get a better understand as to what was really going on. Tony understood that it would be easy for Jermel and his crew to take him down. Tony was very manipulative. He looked at life as you would a game of chess where some pieces are valuable, while others were easily put into position for sacrifice. Tony was smarter at using the pieces around him, always giving himself the advantage in the streets. He was well rounded in all aspects of the drug game. He had been taught by a long line of family at a young age how to handle situations such as the one he faced with Jermel. Though he liked the youngster, he still had to look into the situation to make sure he was safe.

The street lights bounced off the windshield of Jermel's car as he made his way to the I-95 North exit off of New York

Avenue. He had made a couple of stops in DC before he left to go visit Tony. He made sure he stopped to visit Pig's mother before he left. One reason was to talk to her to find out how his arraignment went, and the other was to make sure Pig and Young World's commissary account was full. Jermel knew it was his responsibility to have their back while they were on the inside, as well as on the streets. That's one of the things he'd learned from the old times on 7th St., loyalty is always a must in the streets. Never turn your back on your friends, even at the worst of times.

Jermel smiled as he thought of what Black had done to him when he was younger. Although he wanted a normal life at times, he couldn't discredit the fact that he loved the values the streets had grounded him with.

Jermel was relieved when he saw the sign that read George Washington Memorial Bridge 1 Mile. He traveled there with twenty thousand in cash in the console of the car and his Glock 40. He understood he was taking a big chance driving up there dirty but felt he had no other choice.

He drove to 125th st to the location where he was supposed to meet Tony. It wasn't long before a black 850BMW with dark tint pulled alongside his car. The window slowly came down revealing Tony's face and a Beautiful Dominican woman with flawless skin and long jet black hair in the passenger seat of the car. She looked to be in her early twenties. Tony hit the volume button to turn down the blasting music in the car and told Jermel to follow him.

The traffic was heavy in New York's busy streets. Horns blew as the aggressive drivers dodged in and out of traffic to their preferred destinations. Tony turned on Fifth Ave., with Jermel tagging closely behind. They pulled in front of a tall apartment building on 56st. in the lower Westside. The scenery was a lot different from Uptown Manhattan where they met.

The streets were well kept and there were expensive cars lined on both sides on the street. Tony signaled for him to get out of the car. Jermel noticed that it was a lot colder in New York and decided it was time to put his leather coat on. The sun had just gone down which made the temperature fall a few degrees. Tony waited for him while the girl with him made her way to the lobby of the building looking like a runway model.

"Damn Tony is that your girl?" said Jermel.

"Who her? She just a friend," said Tony.

"I bet you enjoy waking up beside her," said Jermel

"Yo shorty you like her huh? She is my girls little sister. She was only with me because I told her all about you so I asked her to ride with me to meet you. I knew you were going to be with me for a while so I made sure I got you some company," said Tony.

"That's what's up," said Jermel

"I know you been through a lot" said Tony. "I'm going to take you out tonight to have a little fun. Just to take your mind of everything and enjoy yourself. Everything is going to be alright."

"It's hard to have fun when my man is locked up," said Jermel.

"Don't worry; I got it all under control. I got one of the best Jewish lawyers in New York. I already talked to him about you. We got an appointment to see him tomorrow. Trust me, your part of the family and I am going to always make sure family is taken care of, "said Tony

For the first time in a couple of weeks Jermel felt at ease. He cleared his mind and started to look forward to hanging out with Tony while he was in New York. He never went out during his trips there it was mainly about business. Most of the time, he would be in and out in less than 24hours.

They got into the elevator that led to Tony's condo. The first thing he noticed when he entered through the door was all the people that were sitting around listening to their favorite salsa music. The room was filled with five Dominican women. The smell of marijuana lingered in the air as a young woman passed the neatly rolled blunts in rotation. Each one turns to greet him like they knew him for years. Jermel quickly adapted to the environment. He was passed one of the blunts and encouraged by one of the woman to take and relax. Jermel got comfortable by taking his jacket off, inhaling the smoke from the exotic bud that constantly came his way. He enjoyed the hospitality of Tony and the females. They had the best weed and the finest wine one could desire, Jermel wasn't big on drinking and didn't indulge, but he smoked everything that came his way.

The plan was to go out to the famous Club Tunnel. It was located on 27th and 12th in the Manhattan borough. It was known as the hottest club in New York. Everyone from rappers to athletes would come through to show their face. Friday happens to be the day when one of the best D.Js in New York would turn the tables.

When they got there, the crowd was live. Tony led the pack as they went to the entrance and through the doors. Tony knew the owner of the security company at the door. They always let him and whoever that was with him in with no questions asked.

Jermel was amazed by how big the club was. It could at least hold about two thousand people on a slow night. D.J. Clue had everyone in the spot grooving to the sounds of the newest underground rappers. Jermel was feeling the music and was enjoying the new environment.

"Yo lets go on the floor, its mad girls out there," said Tony.

"Lets go," said Jermel. "You ain't said nothing. That's just what I was thinking about."

"Make sure you stay close by," said Tony, "easy to get separated with all these people in here."

The club was nothing like the Go-Gos that Jermel was use to in D.C., this club had people of all nationalities. He quickly could see why they called it the best in New York.

Jermel and Tony maneuvered their way through the crowd until they ended up on the second floor where they saw a display of a large bar. It was circular with about twenty bar stools around it. The bartenders were all young woman with really friendly attitudes. Their uniforms consisted of a white button down shirt exposing cleavage with a short black skirt and four inch heels.

They lounged at the bar for the next hour with Tony downing Remy Martin V.S.O.P one after another. Tony was the total opposite of Jermel. He would always prefer to drink than smoke. Jermel could see that the drinks were starting to get the best of him by the way his speech was starting to slur.

Two young females came by and sat a couple of stools down from them. Both ladies could pass for twenty something. They reminded you of your most common New York hood girls. Both wore skin tight jeans and body shirts. One was 5'6 about 140pounds with a smooth dark complexion. The other was around 120 pounds standing about 5'3; she looked as though she was mixed with two different ethnic groups. She could pass for European or Latin decent.

"Bartender," said Tony. "Let me get another round and give one to the ladies next to me."

"Coming right up," the bartender said.

"Thank you," said the ladies.

"It all good ma," said Tony, "what's your name?" he said

"I'm Jennifer," The dark skinned female replied. "And this is Sasha."

"I'm Tony and this is my man Jermel," said Tony.

Tony took it upon himself to get to know them better. He signaled the bartender to keep the drinks coming their way. Tony started to feel the music as N.W.A. most recent club banger 'It's the world's biggest dick' blast through the speakers. Tony got up dancing to the music while making it behind Jennifer; he put his arms around her hips and started to grind on her aggressively. Jennifer bobbed her head and downed the remains of her drink indicating she was feeling good as well.

Jermel saw the look on Sasha's face as two dudes walked in their direction. One of the dudes was dressed in blue jeans, red champion sweat shirt and red and white Air Force Ones. His man was in an army fatigue uniform with black Timbs.

Jermel could see the discomfort on one of the dudes face, as they walked up to Tony and the girls. Without saying a word the chubby guy dressed in army fatigues wear pushed Tony from behind. Tony didn't know what was going on but responded with a wild punch in direction of the guy. Tony was so drunk he stumbled and fell to the floor. One of the guys kicked him while he was down

"Trey!" yelled Jennifer "leave him alone, you're a fucking trouble maker."

Jermel quickly assisted Tony by sending a hail of punches in the direction of the guy. Jermel had a four inch pocket knife clenched in his left fist with every swing. The fight caused a big disturbance which alerted the clubs security. As security forced its way through the crowd Jermel helped Tony up as the two went the opposite way of the crowd. They headed for the exit of the club. All Jermel was thinking about how he didn't want any run in with the law. As soon as they made it outside Jermel flagged the first cab in sight to Tony's condo. Within the next five minutes Tony was stretched out in the back of the cab sleep.

The next morning Jermel could smell the aroma in the air as Maria prepared breakfast. The smell of the homemade blueberry muffins made him hungry. Jermel looked at the blood spots on his shoes as they laid on the floor. He felt like trouble followed him everywhere he went and wondered when he would get a break.

Maria who Jermel remembered from being with Tony when he met him upon his arrival interrupted his thoughts when she walked in, she gave him a smile and told him breakfast was waiting for him.

He went to the breakfast table which was occupied by Tony, Maria and Sonya; Jermel could see a big red bruise on Tony's face from the altercation at the club.

"Jermel, how's it going?" said Tony.

"Hey what's up," said Jermel.

"Yo homie, I want to thank you for being there for me last night, I had too much to drink I guess and I got carried away," said Tony.

"Don't sweat it," said Jermel, "whenever you're wit me, know that I got your back."

"Yeah, I respect that," said Tony. "You showed me a whole nother side last night. You're the type I need around. I feel much more comfortable around you now. To show my appreciation I want to pay all the legal fees for you and your man."

"You don't have to do that," said Jermel. "We put a little something aside for that."

"That's already paid for," said Tony. "I got on top of that this morning. You don't come across loyal players in this game every day. I cherish that and need you around. I got big plans for us."

"Good looking," said Jermel.

"We got to hurry up and eat because Mr. Bloomberg is expecting us at 11:00 today. He said he already had the case faxed to him and will have a little feedback when we get there," said Tony.

Tony was really feeling the way Jermel responded when they were faced with adversity. Tony was a firm believer that action speaks louder than words. He wasn't aware that even though DC is a small city it still breeds killers at a very young age.

Tony and Jermel got to Mr. Bloomberg's office, the secretary explained to them that Mr. Bloomberg was in a meeting and he would be with them in a minute. They took a seat and waited for the lawyer to call them. One thing Jermel learned from Big John was to always prepare when you're breaking the law in the streets. Trouble is easy to get into but hard to get out of. He called remembrance to Mr. Brown, the family lawyer Big John used since Jermel was a little boy. Big John retained Mr. Brown in advance just in case legal trouble came his way.

Mr Bloomberg came out of his office and welcomed Tony as if he was an old college buddy that he hadn't seen in years, He looked to be in his mid-fifties, with a very slender build. Jermel was expecting to see a man with a very expensive taste from observing the elegance of the office. Mr. Bloomberg was the total opposite wearing a cheap brown suit, black loafers, and a white yarmulke, which was Jewish religious head wear positioned on top of his bald head.

"Tony my friend, you two come in and have a seat," said Mr. Bloomberg, "Would you like a cup of coffee?"

"Thank you Mr. Bloomberg," said Tony. "This is Jermel, the one we've talked about."

"How are you young man?" he said.

"I'm fine," said Jermel.

"Well son, let's get straight to business. You are facing some serious allegations. The bad thing about dealing with the government is that, that's all it takes for them to get a warrant for you arrest," He continued. "They operate off pure presumption. The good thing about law is it requires the government to show factual proof of the presumption to be found guilty."

"Can they do that in my case?" said Jermel.

"From what I know right now, it's going to be very hard, said Mr. Bloomberg. I haven't nearly finished my investigation in your case but I did have the grand jury minutes in your case faxed to me."

"That's the records of the grand jury hearing," said Mr. Bloomberg. "It doesn't look that bad except for a Ms. De'Shawta Mills testimony. She's saying she witnessed five young black males in the act of shooting out at the gas station where she worked. Besides her they got one more witness named James Allen that said he was with you in the case of the gas station incident. So far it's your word against his. The lady from the gas station is only relevant because of his statement."

The meeting lasted about thirty minutes total. After Mr. Bloomberg revealed all that he had gathered from his sources, Jermel asked questions about the next stage of the process.

"I can't believe my little man is snitching," said Jermel.

"In this game you should never be surprised at what someone does," said Tony. "Loyalty and trust is something that's earned not given, it's very easy for someone to say they got your back, some may think in their mind that they're there for you, but pressure bust pipes, remember that," Tony said.

The words that Tony spoke caused Jermel to reflect back to when he was young, Black use to preach the same kind of thing to him. The test the Black put him through came clearly to his mind as if it had just happened. For the first time

Jermel appreciated that experience and now understood the true existence of being loyal and trustworthy.

As they drove away from the lawyers office Tony went on about the importance of knowing and understanding the people you're dealing with in life. Tony even told Jermel that was the main reason he told him to come to New York. He felt like with Jermel being by his side he could get a better understanding of what's going on in DC. Jermel gave him a look of concern as Tony stated its importance. Once again Jeremel heard the words 'It's not personal' that Black told him years ago when he first came into the game. Tony told him you have to protect yourself at all times. That even goes for the ones that are close to you.

Ring . . . ring . . . ring "hello," said Goldie.

"Hey what's up,"? said Jermel.

"Why haven't you called me? I been worried about you and Pig, everything is going to be alright. Tony got us a lawyer out of New York. He got an office in DC also. I just had a meeting with him tell Pig he sending someone from his office down to see him the week," said Jermel.

"OK, Jermel I'll tell him. I'm sure he's going to be glad I talked to you because he has been calling here every day."

"Tell him that Young World ran his mouth to them people too," said Jermel," That's the only solid piece of evidence they got. Tell him he'll see the statement when the lawyer comes to see him. One more thing, I'll be calling more so be looking for my calls. It'll probably be from unknown numbers."

"Alright son, I'll do that and take care of yourself," said Goldie.

CHAPTER 26

Rise and shine said counselor Reed as he walked into the hallway of the unit 7a. He yelled out to all the boys on the floor that they have twenty minutes to get ready for breakfast.

Pig rolled over in the small bed of his single man cell irritated at the fact he had to get up so early in morning. He had been there for nearly three weeks and still hasn't adapted to the transition that he was facing.

After a few moments of dealing with his frustration Pig got out of the last one to come out of his room. By the time he was finish, counselor Reed was instructing the boys to line up single file for a quick count before heading off to the cafeteria to eat breakfast. Pig filled in to the back of the line, now alert and ready for whatever turn of events that came his way.

As always Chase and Young World sat and waited for Pig to arrive. They made sure they got together every morning at breakfast time before they went to the school building. All the boys there had to either get there G.E.D. or take a trade of some sort during their stay at Oakhill.

"What's up cuz," said Chase. "I talked to my mother last night when I made my phone call, she told me to tell you she sends her love, and tell you Goldie said call her as soon as you can", said Chase.

"Alright," said Pig. "What else did she say? "She said she talked to Jermel and he said he got y'all a lawyer. He should be coming to see you in the next few days," Chase explain while eating his cereal that was served that morning.

"I knew Jermel was going to be on top of things," said Pig. "I wonder where he's at. I know the feds is everywhere looking for him."

"Shorty's smart," said Chase. "He ain't going to do anything stupid to get caught up." Young World just sat there in silence, thinking about how it wouldn't be long before they know he cracked under pressure and made that statement to the detectives. Fear entered his body when he realized the repercussions of his actions.

They had many conversations about the importance of being loyal and tru to the game. That was something they build a strong bond upon which should not be broken under any circumstances. Young World's young mind reflected back to the incident that they participated in with Big John. Anxiety overcame him as he pictured how effortless Jermel pulled the trigga and aimed it at the head of his own family member. He knew if it happened to his, he surely could get it as well. Shanita was also on his mind. He was infatuated with everything about her. The way she walks, her demanding nature and furthermore the things she done to him in the bedroom. His flesh was totally dominated by her seduction.

Young world was becoming very stressed as the days went by. It had gotten to the point where his sleep was limited to only a few hours a night. His conscience was eating him alive. He knew it was inevitable that his betrayal would be known. Oppression would soon come his way as a result of his actions.

Pig, Chase, and Young World made plans to get back together later that day on the basketball court. They all had to go to school for a few hours before having free time to hang out.

Although school was designed to prepare the young boys for their G.E.D. or their next grade in school when they return back to society few took advantage of the opportunity. Instead they used that time to shoot dice, share street stories, and flirt with the young female staff that worked in the education department.

The days passed at a fast pace for Pig. It was always something going on at the facility. After another routine day of school, the youngsters made their way back to their assigned units.

Pig was trying to plot on a way to call his mother. It was Tuesday and he wasn't due for another phone call until Friday or Saturday whenever the counselor got around to him. Sometimes if the right counselor was working was working Pig would sneak in the office at night and use the phone while he were watching TV or engaged in a conversation with one of the females that works there.

Pig desperately wanted to know what the word was on the street. He knew Jermel's talk with his mother had more to it than what Chase told him. He just needed to talk to his mother to find out.

After the afternoon count was over Pig walked through the back doors of the unit that led to the basketball courts where he was suppose to meet Chase and Young World.

The boys played 5 on 5 pickup games as Pig approached. The yard was filled do the first day of the good weather for the week. It had been raining and really wet outside prior to this day.

Pig looked around for Chase and Young World. He navigated through the crowded rec yard in search until he saw Chase sitting down while using one of the basketballs as a seat.

"Cuz What's Up?" said Pig walking up.

"Aint shit", said Chase." I been out here for like thirty minutes waiting on ya'll."

"Where's Young World?" said Pig. I told him about this shit already. That little big head motherfucker is getting hard headed by the day.

"I haven't seen him but he will probably be out here shortly," said Chase.

"If them Sheppard St dudes catch him somewhere when we not around it might be problems for him," said Pig. "What's up with the smoke? Anybody got some for sell?" Pig asked.

"The dude Boobie told me he was going to come back and holla at me," Chase replied.

They hung out hoping to get some weed while waiting on Young World to show up. That was their everyday routine, get together after school and smoke weed. Drugs were plentiful due to the amount of crooked counselors that was willing to risk their jobs and possibly legal trouble for the extra money they made from bringing the drugs in.

Pig rolled two small joints out of the bag of marijuana that he got from Boobie on the rec yard. Chase passed Pig the matches from his shoes that he stole from one of the school buildings. Pig lit one of the sticks and passed it to Chase between drags.

Chase attention was drawn when he saw five staff members running to unit 8b. Normally, that means it's a fight taking place or the staff in that unit needed assistance. Chase knew Young World was in that unit and hoped he hadn't gotten into anything.

"They going in unit 8," said Chase,

"I see," Pig replied.

"I hope shawty didn't get into it with none of them dudes," said Chase. "You know he got a big mouth."

"Yea, he talks a lot of shit to be a hundred pounds soak and wet," said Pig. "This is the shit I've been dealing with on the streets. He don't listen to nothing you tell him. If that is him, it wouldn't be happening if he would have been out here like we told him."

"You right Pig, I'm gonna put my foot up his little ass when I see him," Chase said with a serious look on his face.

When all the personnel at the facility entered the unit, counselor Reed directed them to room 14 where Young World was assigned. Counselor Simms rushed in anticipating breaking up a fight that was taking place but instead saw Young World's frail body hanging lifeless from the shoe laces around his neck that he used to commit suicide with. Eyes still open showing he was surprised from the wrath of death.

Chase was devastated by the news and had to be taken to unit 10a away from the population. He loved his little brother and couldn't accept the fact that he was gone. Chase sat in segregation trying to understand why he would to take his own life. Chase was released back to the compound the day of Young World's memorial in the institution. Chase was supposed to read a poem in remembrance of him. The young boys filled the chapel to pay their respects. A picture of Young World sat on table in the front of the chapel as the chaplain gave a brief sermon about the joy of life.

Afterward Pig waited outside the chapel for Chase to come out. He gave him a hug and told him to come with him outside to talk.

"That's messed up shawty did that to himself," said Pig.

"Yea, I know, he was my heart," said Chase

"I talked to my mother and I think I know why he did it," Pig said.

"What you mean, you think you know why he did it?" Chase asked.

"She told me Jermel said Young World was making statements to them people."

"How the fuck he know?" said Chase. "For all I know Jermel might be the fucked up, he's the only one not locked up."

"Hold up cuz you over reacting, the lawyer told him that he got the word on our case," Pig stated.

"Tell Jermel sucka ass I don't believe that and he going to have to see me when I come home," Chase said. "I ain't letting that nigga throw no dirt on my little brother grave."

Pig spent hours trying to reason with Chase but he was so bitter about losing his little brother he just wanted to take his anger out on anybody. Pig knew that put him in a bad position because Jermel was his right hand man and Chase was family. Pig just hoped he could keep them from bumping heads.

The End